THE DEATH CLUB

RICK WOOD

Blood Splatter Press

The Sensitives:

Book One — The Sensitives

Book Two — My Exorcism Killed Me

Book Three — Close to Death

Book Four — Demon's Daughter

Book Five — Questions for the Devil

Book Six - Repent

Book Seven - The Resurgence

Book Eight - Until the End

Shutter House

Shutter House

Prequel Book One - This Book is Full of Bodies

Cia Rose:

Book One — After the Devil Has Won

Book Two — After the End Has Begun

Book Three - After the Living Have Lost

Chronicles of the Infected

Book One — Zombie Attack

Book Two — Zombie Defence

Book Three — Zombie World

Standalones:

When Liberty Dies

I Do Not Belong

Death of the Honeymoon

Blood Splatter Books

Psycho B*tches

Home Invasion

Anthologies

Roses Are Red So Is Your Blood

Twelve Days of Christmas Horror

Twelve Days of Christmas Horror Volume 2

Sean Mallon:

Book One — The Art of Murder

Book Two — Redemption of the Hopeless

The Edward King Series:

Book One — I Have the Sight

Book Two — Descendant of Hell

Book Three — An Exorcist Possessed

Book Four — Blood of Hope

Book Five — The World Ends Tonight

Non-Fiction

How to Write an Awesome Novel

[1]

@LUVVAGIRL99

I LAY UPSIDE DOWN ON MY BED SO PEACEFULLY THAT, IF it weren't for the blood, you wouldn't know I'm dead.

Some of the pills I swallowed are in a lump of sick on my red satin sheets.

Soon it will crust.

Or maybe it won't.

I don't know quite how long it will be until Mum finds me. My body might be stiff by then, it might not. It doesn't really matter. At least not to me. There is no heaven welcoming me home, such a thing is made up to comfort the weak — I didn't exist fourteen years ago, and now I don't exist again.

The webcam light on my laptop still shines, but he doesn't watch anymore.

He's done what he needed to.

The worst part? I wasn't even the main event. The only purpose to my death was practice — a dress rehearsal for the girl he really wanted, and it didn't take him as long as you'd have thought.

You will read my story in the newspaper tomorrow, or

the day after that, or the day after that — but not next week; I will be old news by then.

You will read it and they will think — *how could a girl be so easily manipulated? That would never happen to me.*

In which case, you are an idiot. Of course this could happen to you.

Psychologists say victims are exploited because of vulnerabilities, as that's what makes them the best targets — but aren't we all vulnerable? Don't we all have weaknesses that can be exploited?

I bet you'll also say I was stupid to send pictures, and that you'd never do that; like you're oh so perfect. But it doesn't just happen, does it?

It starts slowly. Begins with flattery. Begins by filling the hole in your life you didn't know was there.

He made me feel good about myself. He knew what my insecurities were and he knew how to quell them, knew how to have me walking around with a smile where there never was one before. Confides in me about things he has never confided in anyone else; or so he says. Like that that time he cried or that time he felt sad or that time he threw his chair across the room in anger.

He never cried or felt sad or threw a chair. Don't be so stupidly naïve. He's just filling a need.

You aren't even aware you needed him, but soon you can't imagine going a day without messaging. You feel loved. Appreciated. Like you're worth something.

Then he isolates you.

He uses all that trust and all that emotional reliance to force his truth into your thoughts — until it is your truth too, and you are doing what he wants without even knowing it.

You'll never know his real name, but you don't need to. Give him anyone's.

My body starts to smell as his last message disappears from the screen. On his side of the webcam, he is already wiping away the evidence. He is already creating a clean slate that will have everyone believe I succumbed to weakness. That this life was too much for me and I couldn't survive.

It was an overdose, but that only tells a small part of the story.

My empty body is evidence of a troubled girl, but evidence skews perceptions, it does not support it.

It's time for somebody else's story now. My part is done. I set the scene. I let you know what happened to me so you know what will happen to the next girl.

I gave you an insight to my life long after I took it away.

But don't be fooled.

Don't think this is what it looks like.

See, you may think this is suicide, but you're wrong — make no mistake my friends, this was murder.

Nothing more.

And nothing less.

[2]

WILL

It's 8:30p.m. and I'm already in bed, listening to Harper's footsteps in the kitchen. You know you're pathetic when you go to bed before your teenage daughter.

The bed is king size, and it feels empty without Natalie, but I'm listening out for her. Waiting until she stumbles through the door, swearing as she searches for a light switch, so I can rush down and hold her hair back as she throws up in the toilet.

It's safe to say that I failed at marriage fairly epically. We were twenty when we met. Second year of university. Teacher training. Only I went on to qualify, and she...

Even back then, the problems started, yet I couldn't see them.

I close my eyes and the house descends into silence. Harper's bedroom door closes and her steps no longer patter around. The house remains peaceful until I'm woken up shortly after 1.00a.m. by a clatter against the front door. I leap from the bed, rush out the room, and take the steps two at a time, hoping I can avoid Harper being woken up by the commotion.

When I open the door, Natalie has already thrown up on the porch. She has half a kebab in one hand and clutches onto a ripped clutch bag in the other. Her mascara is smeared across her eyes and the strap of her dress falls low enough down her arm that her bright pink bra is exposed.

"Are you okay?" I ask. She pushes me out the way and stumbles in, falling to the floor, and what do I sort out first, the vomit or my wife?

Sometimes I wonder if she regrets this in the morning, but I'm never around to find out as I'm at work, ready to teach, ready to convince myself I'm inspiring the next generation while a group of disinterested adolescents determine that I am the exact kind of person they do not wish to grow up to be.

With my arm around her, gripping onto her sweaty shoulder, I help her up the stairs, one at a time, keeping her steady as she wobbles. I cover her mouth when we pass Harper's room and she just smacks it away.

"Who were you with?" I ask, once I've closed the bedroom door behind us. "Was it Brian?"

She says nothing.

"It was, wasn't it? It was Brian."

She mumbles something and, despite its incoherence, I take it as confirmation.

"I'm sick of that guy," I say, under my breath.

She falls over. I steady her and help her on the bed. Take off her dress. Notice something on her neck. It looks like a hickey. Hell, it could just be a rash.

I place the duvet over her like I used to do with Harper when she was younger. Back when my daughter respected me. Back when she would be happy to call me Dad. Now, she hardly calls me anything. She doesn't even get angry with me. I hate it. Nothing's more painful than indifference.

I stroke Natalie's hair as she falls asleep and try to see the woman I met when we were young. She was always wild, but wild is okay in your youth. Your twenties are about self-exploration. But it gets to a point in your life when wild is no longer fun. Being a party animal becomes being an alcoholic. I always thought that, once I outgrew the night life, so would she.

Being a mother changed her initially. But not for long.

Then again, did it change her? Or was I just seeing what I wanted to see?

I would see her reading the parenting books when she was pregnant and smile, then convince myself I was mistaken when she snuck herself sips of vodka from the fridge. She would make my friends laugh during games night, then refill another glass of wine and make inappropriate, vulgar comments. She would look me in the eyes and tell me she loved me, and I would use those three words to cover up any evidence that showed otherwise.

So how did she become *this*? At what point did it go from bad to worse, and could I have done something to stop it?

Or was it always this bad, and I just couldn't face up to it?

I leave the bedroom. Trudge down the stairs. The bleach is in the front of the cupboard for easy access. I take it, enter the porch, get on my hands and knees and scrub.

It's beginning to rain, and I could probably leave it to the elements to clean the sick away — but I want to be sure it's gone. Harper can't see this. I can't let her.

Maybe things would be different if I'd been a better husband. Spent more time talking to Natalie instead of marking books. I always tried, but maybe I didn't try hard enough.

Once I'm done, I hide the cleaning equipment away, and I squeeze handwash into my palms and hold them under the tap, watching the water cascade between the cracks of my fingers, turning them over and over. I do this four times. Always four, never more, never less. Four has always comforted me. I'm not sure why. When I was a child, there was me, my sister and my parents — four of us. It felt like a solid unit. Like we were impenetrable.

But now I'm in a family of three.

I make my way back upstairs and pause outside Harper's room. There is no movement.

She hasn't heard any of it.

I return to bed, and allow myself a few hours of light sleep.

[3]

HARPER

I DON'T MOVE FROM BENEATH THE DUVET. IT'S A double quilt on a single bed, and it's the warmest thing in the house, and I'm safe in here.

Mum's drunk again. I know it.

We never talk about it, but I know it.

I hear Dad shushing her, but he can do nothing to hide the chaotic steps up the stairs, pounding the ground like misplaced notes in a poorly written symphony. There is no rhythm to Mum's steps when she's drunk, only disorder.

It gets cooler when he goes outside. He seems to stay there for a while. I don't know what he's doing. I don't hear the car leave, and I don't hear the front door close, but I feel the cold it lets in.

Sometimes I pretend to have a normal family. We could still be dysfunctional, but in an endearing way, like families you see in sitcoms, like *Malcolm in the Middle* or *The Simpsons*, where their dysfunctionality makes them normal.

But our dysfunctionality is not normal. I never see anyone in these sitcoms with a mother who's an alcoholic.

Never.

Sometimes I wonder what my friend's families would be like, should I have any friends. I see other mums and dads on parent's evening, sitting with their child. Sometimes I even see a dad with a notepad, writing stuff the teachers say down.

The only thing Dad ever brought to my parent's evening was shame.

Eventually, I hear him plodding up the stairs, keeping his footsteps light, but unable to hide the sadness from the way he walks. I always know who's coming up or down the stairs from the sound of their walk. Mum's used to be with the clip clop of her slippers, and Dad's used to be with a spritely bounce.

Now they are ominous, foreboding stamps, only Dad tries to lighten the impact of his.

He pauses outside my room. I don't know what he's doing, maybe checking if I'm awake, and I stay as still as I can.

Not that he'd hear me anyway, but I don't take any chances.

Then the steps disappear, his bedroom door shuts, and the house is peaceful again.

This is the only time when the house is peaceful, and I often lay awake, relishing it. I get tired at school and my teachers get annoyed when they have to wake me up in class, but I'm not really bothered. There's nothing that any of them can teach me that would make home more bearable.

At least I'm ignored, I suppose. It would be worse if Mum or Dad pretended to give a shit. I'd rather be left alone in my room, silent in our agreement that we don't interfere with each other's lives.

I think I'm better off alone. Sometimes I picture my future, and I have my own house, and I work alone at my own business, and I spend my weekends walking alone in a forest, maybe with a dog.

It's a beautiful image.

It's silent in this image, too.

And silence is something I often dread, yet am all too grateful for when it arrives.

[4]

WILL

When my alarm goes, I'm already awake. To be honest, I've been awake for an hour, listening to my wife's gentle snoring, appreciating the calmness. I'm tempted to put an arm around her, but I don't; she is on her side, facing away from me, so I stay on my side of the bed like there's an invisible wall between us.

I sit up and turn off the alarm.

"Honey," I say with a hushed voice. "Honey, are you awake?"

She gives a slight groan.

"It's morning. I'm going to make breakfast; would you like any?"

She ignores me.

"Honey?"

She still ignores me.

"I said, I'm going to make—"

"Fuck off."

I wait for her to say something else. Sometimes she opens her eyes and complains about her hangover. A few years ago she even apologised. Now, however, she does nothing. Her eyes stay closed and she doesn't move.

I'd like to say her reaction surprises me, but I'm not even phased by it.

I get up, walk quietly downstairs and into the kitchen. When Natalie's hangovers are really bad, she doesn't like to eat too much. No bacon or sausages or waffles; just toast. So that's what I make her. Lightly browned, not too burnt, and with a thin layer of margarine. I return to the bedroom with said toast and a cup of black coffee, and set them on the table beside her.

"There's some toast for you here," I say, still with a hushed voice.

After waiting for a reaction that doesn't come, I make my way into the ensuite, close the door, and masturbate silently in the shower. I think of Natalie on top of me, riding away, screaming with pleasure. The image is old and grainy now, and I'm not sure I can remember the contours of her body quite like I used to, but it's enough to see me through to orgasm. Then I stand still until I'm limp and wash myself with soap. I used to use shower gel, but Natalie's allergic.

My brown suit is hanging lifelessly in the cupboard. I put it on with a grey shirt and survey my ties. Each one is comical in some way; like the tie covered in hearts or the one with characters from *Family Guy* or the one covered in footballs. People always seem to buy me ties. Barely a birthday or Christmas goes by without it. It's always my sister or my mum. It's the present you get a man when you don't know what else to get him.

Natalie used to give me a tie on anniversaries, but not so much anymore.

I choose a black one with red dots and glance back at Natalie. Her toast must have gone cold by now.

When I return to the kitchen, I find Harper sat at the counter making her way through a small bowl of Coco Pops.

"Good morning," I say.

She glances up at me and grunts.

In a way, she is the ideal daughter. Unlike so many of the teenage girls I teach, she is happy to wear a skirt that goes down to her ankles, to carry around a big backpack, and to wear large glasses like the kind my dad used to wear in the nineties.

Then again, sometimes I wish she would rebel a bit more. Would be a bit more normal.

No, I don't mean *normal*. That's a horrible thing to say.

Just more...

Someone who fits in. Not for my sake, I don't care that she's an outcast — I just worry that she's never going to make any friends. And I don't mean the friends she makes online, when she sits on the computer for hours on those message boards; I mean *real* friends. She has never asked to go to a sleepover, or for me to drop her into town to meet someone, or if she could go to a party. If she came home drunk one night, I'd probably be grateful she had someone to get drunk with.

Then again, maybe I should be grateful she has so little of her mother in her.

"Would you like a lift to school?" I ask.

"No thanks."

"Are you sure? I don't mind, you don't have to walk—"

"I said no thanks."

Sometimes I wonder where I went wrong. When did I mess up my marriage so badly, and what did I do to make my daughter hate me?

At least I'm trying.

"Would you like me to pick you up at least?"

"I said no."

"I really don't mind."

She doesn't look up.

"Okay. Right, well, have a good day. I will see you this evening."

I smile at her, though she won't see it, and I take the box of books I was supposed to mark and make my way to my plain grey Mitsubishi Mirage. The gear stick gets stuck as I try to move into reverse, but a little force helps, and I back down the drive of a house I bought ten years ago with all the love and aspiration a family man could ask for, and ignore the overgrown weeds that surround it.

HARPER

A LIFT.

He offers me a lift.

Like a dad would.

Like it makes up for anything.

I want to say to him, "Why are you so pathetic? Why do you pretend that you can lift your head up high? Why don't you admit what you are?"

But I don't.

Mum already tells him. I hear her, sometimes. When they think I'm asleep, or not listening, or when I have my headphones in but my music off.

They think I hear nothing, but I hear everything.

When I'm around, they don't talk, like they think the silence spares me the arguments, but the silence is even worse. At least when they are arguing there's passion behind it; when they are silent, it's like they are dead.

He finally leaves and he finally stops talking to me, and I drag myself to the front door, hoisting a bag full of books and folders over my shoulders, and make my way out. I see my reflection in the window, and the weight of my bag is making me hunch over. I don't know how everyone else at school manages with their little handbags or tiny rucksacks.

Then again, they are the ones who always ask to borrow a pen, because they don't bring anything with them in those tiny bags. And it's always me they ask.

I approach the school and it's full of eyes and full of faces and I try not to look at any of them. Some people laugh and I don't understand how they can enjoy being here so much. As soon as I am among the crowds of students wearing the same school uniform, I feel like I'm in the middle of a zoo and surrounded by predators.

I walk through the corridor with my head down and I hear sniggering and I wonder if it's at me. It's like they all look at me yet no one notices me. I am invisible, yet I feel like I stand out.

A girl barges into me. She doesn't even flinch. She carries on laughing, holding hands with a boy just as pretty as she is.

I walk into an IT classroom for registration, take my seat on my own at the back, and avoid making eye contact with anyone. My tutor talks but I don't hear anything. She gives some letters out and one drops on my table but I don't pay attention to it.

When registration is over I wait for everyone else to leave so I can go. My tutor says hello and I try to smile though I know my lips barely move.

In science, we are told to get into twos or threes for an experiment. No one comes to join me, and I look away from anyone who walks past. I end up working on my own, and either the teacher doesn't even notice, or they do and they choose to let me so they don't have to force anyone to go in a group with me.

She forced Charlene to go in a group with me once. I

hated it. She hated it. She told me I was ratchet, and I don't even know what that means. I thought ratchet was a cog, and she laughed when I didn't look up to meet her stare.

For a moment, I look forward to being able to go home.

Then I remember what home is like.

And I look forward to nothing.

[6]

WILL

On the way to work I get stuck behind a tractor, and a large queue of cars continually honk their horns at me. I'm not sure why their aggression is aimed at me, as it's a twisty road and there is nowhere for me to overtake, yet the gestures made by the fella riding the bumper of my car makes it quite clear what he thinks of the situation.

I end up pulling over into a layby to let him pass, and receive a middle finger out his window. I'm not sure what I was meant to do, but I try not to think about it as I join the large queue of cars from the opposite end.

I tune into the local radio. There is a news report of a teacher in Manchester who has been suspended pending investigation. I turn the volume up.

"A fifteen-year-old female student has made allegations that her geography teacher attempted to kiss her. Police are currently investigating the matter but, like many similar situations, it appears that it's going to come down to his word against hers."

I shake my head. The fool. That is why you keep your

classroom door open if alone with a student, and ensure there is a space between you and them.

"Despite the teacher, twenty-eight-year-old Patrick Armidge, vigorously denying the accusation, he says he has already been the subject of abuse. Police have confirmed that, over the weekend, eggs were thrown at his house and a firework put through his letterbox."

I flinch. In a way, I feel sorry for the guy. He hasn't been found guilty yet, but not only will his career already be over, and not only will the media be camped on his lawn, he is being persecuted for something he may not even have done.

Then again, I don't feel that sorry for him. Guilty or not, it is a situation he could have avoided.

"The girl, who cannot be named because of her age, has been suspended from the school numerous times. Her parents have condemned the actions of her teacher, and do not wish to comment further."

So it was a vulnerable child as well; one that a teacher knew he should be careful with.

I turn the radio off. It's men like him who make a mockery of the teaching profession.

I arrive at school, and search for a space in an over-crowded car park. The only one I can find is between a jeep and a van, but I manage to fit, even if I have to slither through a small gap to get out.

I cross the field to the entrance to the maths block. As I do, Tyler, a delinquent I despise teaching, says, "Hello Mr Coady."

"Hello, Tyler."

As soon as I've passed he says, "Goodbye, bender," and his group of mates snigger and cackle like it's the funniest thing they've ever heard.

I consider going back. Reprimanding him. Telling him off. Reporting it.

But what then?

He'd laugh in my face. With my back turned, I can pretend I didn't hear it.

By the time I get to my classroom it's already left my thoughts. I sit at my laptop, open my emails, and find an email from the headmaster requesting a meeting during my only free period of the day.

Looks like I won't be able to plan any lessons this afternoon.

[7]

HARPER

Lunch time comes and I'm so used to sitting on my own in the canteen that no one even teases me about it anymore. I'm on the edge of a six-seater table, and some-times people take chairs without asking so they can crowd around a smaller table with their friends.

In my lunch box I find dry bread, supermarket own brand salt and vinegar sticks, and a soft banana. I don't remember packing it, then I realise — this was Friday's lunch that I didn't eat.

Still, I'm hungry, so I start nibbling on the bread.

Someone laughs.

I ignore it.

But I can't. They are laughing at me. I look up, and it's a group of girls from the year above, sixteen-years-old and happy, looking and pointing and giggling with each other, and I don't know why they are being mean to me when I've never been mean to them.

"Look at her," I hear one of them say.

"Look at that skirt," says another

Their skirts are black and tiny. Mine is grey and long. I

feel stupid that my socks are pulled up. I feel stupid that I'm wearing glasses. I feel stupid that my hair is pulled back, that I'm eating a dry slice of bread, that my bag is so big.

"She eats like a squirrel."

That did it. That was the observation that turned the giggles to hysteria. They practically fall over each other. One of the guys on the table next to them looks over to see what they are laughing at. One of them just points at me and he grins.

I pick up my lunch box and march through the corridors with my head down until I reach the toilets.

It stinks of urine and it doesn't help my appetite. The lock on two of the doors is broken, so I enter the one with a working lock and shut myself in. There is no toilet lid, so I perch on the seat, and that is where I eat my lunch.

Sitting here makes me feel sick, and the way the bread dissolves in my mouth makes me want to gag.

The floor is slippery. Toilet paper and tampons poke out of the bin. On the wall someone has graffitied a phone number next to the word *slut*.

I wonder what that girl did to deserve it.

At least I'm alone. At least no one will disturb me here. At least I'm locked away and no one can see me.

Most girls seem to want to be noticed.

I can't think of anything worse.

[8]
WILL

WALKING TO THE HEADMASTER'S OFFICE MAKES ME feel like I'm twelve years old all over again, like I've messed around in class or had my shirt untucked or hurt someone playing football. Not that I ever did any of those things, but I always seemed to get the blame.

It's like that prayer. The one about walking through the valley of the shadow of death. It sounds extreme, but it's just how this school feels. The walls are a disgusting cream colour, I can hardly walk a few steps without seeing peeling paint, and the carpet is blue and fluffy, with tufts sticking up and pieces of gum engrained in it.

I pass classrooms where students sit in neat rows of desks, dead-eyed and empty faced. If I walked through a prison, I'm not sure it would look much different.

I see students I know on the way. They shuffle past, avoiding my eye contact, or engrossed in their phones. They should be in lessons, and I know I should stop and ask them why they are wandering around school or have their phones out — especially considering we have a phone ban during lesson time. But what's the point? I don't remember these student's names, so if they refuse, I'd have no way to follow it up as I won't know who they are. And even if I did know their name, I'd find out their identity and pursue their disobedience and their punishment would probably just be a quiet word by their tutor. It's not worth the fuss.

I enter the small lobby that leads to the headmaster's office. I go to knock on the door, but a voice stops me.

"Do you have an appointment?"

To the left is a small office where the headmaster's secretary sits. Her voice is whiny and makes my head throb.

"Yes, he asked to see me," I say, annoyed that I'm being treated like a student. I am a teacher, an adult, I can knock on the head's door myself — but no, his secretary who's on less pay than I am somehow has the power to make me stop and wait.

"What's your name?"

"Will Coady."

"Take a seat and I'll let him know you're here."

I consider not doing as she asks. I consider knocking and walking in. I consider telling her to stuff her seat up her arse.

Then I take a seat and wait.

She picks up the phone and I try to tune her voice out, not wanting the migraine it will probably create. After a few seconds, she puts the phone down and says, "Okay, you can go on in."

With a sigh that prompts a scowl in this woman's face — not that you can see much expression beneath the makeup — I walk into the head's office.

"Will," he says, without looking up. "Please sit down, I will only be a minute."

I sit opposite his desk. Waiting.

He is typing something, and hasn't even looked at me yet.

"Just one moment," he says again, still not looking up.

He takes longer than a moment.

My eyes wander around the office. It's probably the nicest room in the building. Chairs with cushions, new carpet, decent paint job. Qualifications in frames are hung on the wall, which is odd, as I've only ever seen such things in a doctor's office.

"Right," the headmaster says, and types a few more things, then finally turns to me. "Will. How are you?"

"Fine."

His smile is insincere. He is bald, but has evidently tried to deny middle age by going to the gym, such is his physique.

I try to remember his name.

I can't.

"Thank you for coming to see me," he says. "I guess I'll get straight to the point."

He leaves a gap in conversation like I'm meant to say something. I don't.

"I have concerns, Will, and I'm going to be completely honest with you, we have come to the point where I am having to speak to you."

"Oh?"

"Your head of department has flagged up to me that your student's grades are down. As you know, she already highlighted you as a cause for concern earlier in the year, and has been observing some of your lessons."

She has. Every now and then she pokes her pointed face in and sits at the back, watching me, judging me, while I wonder who the hell she thinks she is. She's in her twenties and has only been teaching for a few years. Am I meant to care about her opinion?

"She is still concerned, Will."

He uses my name like he wants me on his side. Repeating it like he's using some kind of technique that will make me like him.

I hate him. He's made teachers redundant, citing lack of funds, then driven home in his flashy BMW. He is everything that is wrong with education.

"Unfortunately, her concerns have now been elevated to me. If we don't see improvements, then we are going to have to go down the route of issuing formal warnings. You understand?"

I nod.

"We expect to see more in your lessons. We expect the learning objectives to be shown, we expect differentiation to be explicit to anyone who enters the classroom, and we expect your student's behaviour to be better. They shouldn't be just passively quiet, but be actively involved. You understand the difference, don't you, Will?"

Stop using my name.

"Yes."

I've been teaching for sixteen years.

Sixteen damn years.

And here is a man telling me how I should do my job.

But do I say this? Do I voice my opinion? Do I let the headmaster know what I think of his warning and expectations?

Do I hell.

"Do you have any questions, Will?"

"No."

"I really would appreciate some more dialogue from

you. I don't want to sit here lecturing you; I would like to have some feedback, to know what your thoughts are."

I say nothing.

"I mean, do you have anything to say about this situation?"

"I don't really know what to say."

"Right. Okay then."

He leans back. Looks at me. Like he's thinking deeply. He wanted more conversation, he wanted me to say more, he wanted this meeting to go differently. Perhaps he expected more fight from me; perhaps he even desired it.

I'm afraid I'm out of fight.

I'm tired and I'm angry and I just want to go to my classroom and plan my lessons.

"Okay, Will, well I will speak to you again, and we hope to see some improvements."

"Thanks," I say as I get up, and I wonder why I said it. It's just automatic, isn't it? You end a meeting and you say thank you.

But why?

I'm not appreciative of anything he's just said.

"Have a good day," he says.

I flash a forced smile and shuffle out.

The secretary says something as I leave, but I ignore her, and I walk back through the ominous corridors to my classroom, where I sit alone and plan lessons and try not to wonder how I got to this point.

[9]

HARPER

After lunch I have textiles. We had to choose one technology to do for our GCSEs, and I could have chosen food technology, graphic design, electronics, woodwork, or textiles. I chose textiles because it's a female-only class, so I figured I could be left alone there, and without the boys to show off to the girls might not be so nasty.

I was wrong.

It is the bitchiest class I've ever known. It is an hour of my day spent listening to girls moan about other girls, and the worst part is that the teacher even joins in. She comes to school wearing short dresses and with her long, blond hair flowing behind her, and, because she's probably closer to our age than she is to most other teachers, she seems to think she's one of us.

The other girls love her. I don't. She does nothing when the other girls turn their attention to me, like she's unable to see that their ruthless comments may be more than just little jokes.

And I can't handle it today. I just can't.

I don't know what it is about today, I just don't want to face that class.

Having skipped her class before and gotten away with it, I decide to do it again. The lunch bell rings and I wait ten minutes for the commotion to go, then I leave the toilets, leave the corridor, and leave the school. No one stops me as I walk through the gates.

I doubt anyone cares.

My textiles teacher probably doesn't even notice that, when she marks me present on the register, that the small piece of silence that sits in the corner isn't even there.

I remember parent's evening when she looked at me, and I could see it in her eyes, that look of confusion as she tried to remember who I am. She had a pile of books and, as we sat down, she said, "Why don't you find your book for me?"

She pretended this was to go through my book with my dad. Really, it was so she could look at the name on the book and know what to call me.

I considered picking the wrong book to see if she'd notice, but I didn't.

It takes twenty minutes or so to walk home. By this point of the afternoon, Mum is normally at the pub or still passed out upstairs. The house is quiet and I am able to sneak inside without anyone knowing I shouldn't be there.

I logon to the computer. The home page on the internet browser shows a few headlines, one about a father and daughter my age found dead, and another about some teacher whose student has accused him of doing dodgy stuff.

I type in the beginning of the web address and the browser fills in the rest. It's called *Hope and Chances*. It's a fan site for fantasy novels and films, though I mainly just use the message board.

This is a place where I'm happy to speak. Where I'm not silent. Where I am noticed. A place where I can be sociable without showing my face. Where I can make friends without the worry of them knowing who I am.

There are a number of forums on the message board I can click on, but I have my favourites. They are *Come to the Café*, a board where you can chat about anything; *Fairies, Fantasies and Frollocks*, where you can share your own interest in fantasy creatures; and *Our Members*, where members can share things that have happened to them.

I go into *Our Members*, and the first post was done an hour ago, but already has 146 replies.

I click on it and read.

Author: @HappyGoLucky_11
Subject: The Death Club

Hi guys,

You may or may not be aware that one of our members, known mainly to you as @LuvvaGirl99, has been in the news today. Turns out her name was Linda Salborough, and it's pretty tragic.

Apparently her dad was found dead, and there are suggestions that the post-mortem found cyanide in his system. Linda herself was also found dead on her bed, apparent suicide by overdose.

Thing is though… I'm not so sure she did kill herself. I mean, I heard her webcam filmed her doing it, and yes she did do it, but I wonder if she was MADE to do it.

Have any of you guys ever heard of something called THE DEATH CLUB?

It's this thing where this anonymous person apparently gets you to kill someone you know then kill yourself on webcam, then he sells the video on the dark web. It's pretty grim, and I don't know why someone would agree to it, but I've heard there are loads of videos doing the rounds. I'm just worried that Linda had something like this happen to her. I don't know.

Hey, this is the internet, so I'm sure many of you will be willing to share your conspiracy theories. Please just be respectful. She was a great member of our community and I know we all wish her family the best.

RIP Linda. Sorry you felt you had to do this.

I feel really sad. I remember @LuvvaGirl99, she replied to a lot of my posts, and we were friendly in a way. She seemed like a really nice person.

I add my comment to the bottom of the post:

Author: @SmallGirl22

Subject: RE The Death Club

Really sorry to hear this. RIP Linda, you were too good for us all.

I click post and I pause, for a moment, then go to the kitchen for a glass of water, still thinking about her. It's sad that someone feels the need to take their own life, but I understand, in a way. Sometimes it feels like the only escape from pain is death. When school is horrible, home is horrible, and inside my head is horrible, the only way to stop it all is to end it. I often wonder whether the world is better off without me.

Then I realise the world doesn't care enough to be better off without me.

Nothing would change. Nobody would notice the empty seat where I used to sit. I doubt anyone would even recognise my name.

I've considered it before. A few times.

I wouldn't hang myself; that would be too painful. I'd overdose. Like Linda did. End it quickly. Hopefully I'd pass out before the pain arrived.

This is not a world for people like me.

I finish my glass of water and place the glass in the bowl. I notice a few empty wine bottles poking out of the bin. I ignore them and return to the computer.

I've already had six comments on my post.

They all seem to be from the same person.

And they all seem to say the same thing.

Author: @PussyMagnet69
Subject: RE RE RE The Death Club

Wht da fuck you know about it?

Author: @PussyMagnet69
Subject: RE RE RE REThe Death Club

Probly just some middle-class stuck-up bitch who likes to pretend to feel bad bout someone else.

Author: @PussyMagnet69
Subject: RE RE RE RE REThe Death Club

You deserve to be fucking raped.

I don't want to read on.

I deserve to be raped?

Who writes that?

I've heard things like this said to me by boys at school, horrible things, but somehow this feels worse…

I've been on this message board for years.

This is where I've made friends.

This is where I belong.

How could someone say something like this?

I go to close the browser. Then I read the rest of the messages.

Author: @PussyMagnet69
Subject: RE RE RE RE RE RE The Death Club

Hope your crying you fucking slut.

Author: @PussyMagnet69
Subject: RE RE RE RE RE RE REThe Death Club

Don't pretend to give a shit. You probly just a stupid cunt with tiny fkin tits you fkin slut.

Author: @PussyMagnet69
Subject: RE RE RE RE RE RE RE REThe Death Club

Don't comment on shit u dnt know. Fk off.

I want to cry.

I want to find this person and scream at them that I do

care, that I'm not stuck-up, that I do understand what it's like to be lonely, to be sad, to want to end things.

But I don't.

I close the browser. Close down the computer. Then sit. And stare.

How could someone write something like that?

It sounds silly, I know, but it's like my home's been destroyed. Like the only place that I can go to get away from everything is now ruined. Tainted. Ripped away from me.

I wipe my eyes. Shut myself in my room. Tell the world to go away, and daydream about how I would end it.

Daydream about what it would be like to no longer exist.

[10]

WILL

LAST PERIOD GOES BY SLOWLY. MY YEAR ELEVENS HAVE
their exams in a few months and we go through a previous
year's exam paper, which is immensely boring, even for me,
and they sit there in tired silence, everyone in daydreams as
I drone on.

The bell goes and I dismiss them and I sit at my desk
and stare at my emails and ignore them. No one says goodbye, or thank you, or see you tomorrow. They all file out in
desperation to get home or meet their friends or do whatever it is they wish to do.

I barely even notice the girl who waits behind.

"Hi, sir," she says, and her voice is sultry, too deep for
her age. Just like many other girls in the class, her skirt is too
short, and she's pulled it up to her navel to make it even
shorter. Her top button is undone, as is the second and
third, and her tiny tie only just covers a glimpse of her bra.

It is incredibly inappropriate, but what am I meant to
do? I was told that I should correct students on their
uniforms, and tell girls when their skirts are too short, but
there's not a chance I'm going to do that. Imagine if a

student took such a comment out of context. Imagine what kind of accusations could be thrown at me. I refuse to do it.

"Hi," I reply, noticing that she is staring at me in a really odd way, like her eyes are transfixed. She keeps smiling and it highlights her freckles. Her hair is long and red and she holds her bare arms behind her back like she's presenting her body to me. Boys her age must go crazy for her.

"I enjoyed your lesson," she tells me.

I try to recall her name, then remember it's Destiny, and I think the same thing I thought when I first saw her name on the register at the beginning of the year — what a ridiculous name. Why can't parents just give their kids actual names? What's wrong with Sally and Kirsten and Jenny and Elizabeth — why do they have to give them made-up names like Destiny or Serenity or Peace. As soon as I look on the register and see someone with a name like that, I know they are going to be annoying.

"I'm glad," I say, wondering why she is still here.

"I just wanted to say that I'm pleased to have you as my teacher," she says. "You are quite inspiring."

"Inspiring?" This girl can't be for real. "We were just going through a test; not sure I'd call it inspiring."

"It wasn't the test, sir. It was you. There's something about you that makes me think I'm going to do really well."

I don't know what the hell this girl is seeing, but it clearly is not in this reality.

"Well," I reply, trying to find something to say, "I'm glad you feel that way."

"I was just wondering..."

"Yes?"

"What made you want to become a teacher?"

I stare at her. Bemused. She looks so eager, so desperate to talk to me. She rests all of her weight on one foot, tilting her head to one side. Her finger rises from behind her waist and fiddles with a loose strand of hair.

"I, erm... I don't know, to be honest."

I became a teacher because I didn't know what else to do. I have regretted it most days since. I don't know what this girl wants from me.

"You best be getting home, I imagine," I say.

"Oh, no, my mum doesn't get home until way later, she works all day. She's a paediatrician. She split up with my dad and said I have to change my surname to her maiden name."

"I'm sorry to hear that."

She shrugs. "It's fine. I prefer seeing my dad on weekends. It makes it more special, you know?"

I lean back. Chew the end of my pen. Wonder how I can get this girl out of my classroom.

"I do have some work to do now, Destiny. It was nice to talk to you."

She smiles. A really wide, big smile.

"You really mean that?"

"Mean what?"

"That it was nice to talk to me."

"Sure," I muster.

Her body moves back and forth, like she's unknowingly doing a little dance of happiness.

"Well, it was very nice to talk to you too, sir."

I force a smile.

"I will see you tomorrow," I say, once again hoping I can prompt her to leave.

"Okay," she says. "I'll look forward to it."

And she finally leaves.

What a strange girl, I think — then I retrieve a load of books and begin marking.

[11]

HARPER

AN ALERT PINGS ON MY PHONE.

I have another reply to my comment.

I don't want to look at it. I don't want to go back on that message board ever again. But curiosity tempts me, and see that I have a reply from a different user.

Author: @HeyThere01
Subject: RE RE RE The Death Club

Wow. I am ever so sorry to hijack this thread, and I am sorry if this is too forthright, @SmallGirl22 — but @PussyMagnet69 appears to be an absolute bellend.

Firstly, let's start on your username. I could forgive the blatant and unfunny use of 69 in your username if it weren't for the preceding claim that you are a pussy magnet.

*In truth, I do not imagine you to be a pussy magnet.
Honestly, I picture you either as a middle-aged man with
little hair who hasn't had sex in at least six years, or a
pre-pubescent child who probably isn't old enough to
know what a 'pussy' actually is.*

*Secondly, I think you should learn to write before you
throw accusations around. Your use of 'your' instead of
'you're' in the 'Hope your crying' part of your message
does not only demonstrate your lack of ability to use the
English language, it also indicates that you must have an
IQ almost low enough to rival anyone with a mental
deficiency.*

*Lastly, your comments are needlessly vile and abusive
and can only suggest that you are some sort of
psychopath. @SmallGirl22 was giving her sincere
condolences on what is a tragedy that has affected all of
us, and your treatment of her can only lead one to
conclude that you are a monstrous, nasty, piece of shit,
who does not deserve the oxygen you are granted.*

*Go back to jacking off, you complete tool, and don't
reduce this message board to bullying. No one cares
about what you have to say.*

I can't help but smile.

I don't know who this guy is, but he has left a huge grin
on my face.

No one has ever stuck up for me before.

Ever.

And here he is, not only telling this horrible, nasty person where to go, but doing it in such a smart way that there is surely no comeback.

He didn't just put him down, he tore him to shreds.

And this stranger will have no idea how happy I am.

I want to message him. I want to say thanks. I want to say something. I want to tell him what he did was cool, and that I can't believe he did it, and… and a million other ways of saying thank you.

I click on his username, then click on a button that says *send private message*, then my thumb hovers…

What do I say?

I've never private messaged anyone before.

I consider backing out of it, but I can't. When someone is this nice, you can't just leave it. I have to say something.

I take a big, deep breath and type.

Hey.

Just wanted to say thank you. So much. That guy really bothered me and I'm really grateful.

You made me smile.

Harper

I sound like a dork.

I hit send before I can change my mind.

Then I stare at the message.

And I feel stupid.

It is a really pathetic message.

You made me smile? I actually wrote that?

What was I thinking?

And I can't delete it now. It's done.

God, I'm ridiculous.

I stand up. Huff. Feeling awful again. Feeling like I just want to be buried in the ground and—

A ping.

He's replied.

I open it, quickly.

Glad I could make you smile ;)

My breath catches.

Then I get another reply.

So how are you, anyway?
Danny.

His name is Danny.

And he wants to know how I am.

I picture him. Short, brown hair. Tall. Good dresser.

I know that may not be what he looks like, but it still intimidates me. He wants to talk to me, and he has no idea how pathetic I am. If he knew, he wouldn't bother sticking up for me. He wouldn't bother asking how I am.

At first, I decide not to reply. Then I think... what if he's a nice guy? What if he's not like any of the kids at school?

What if he's actually genuine, and wouldn't mind it if I'm a dork?

I pick up my phone. Click reply.

Butterflies flutter around my belly. I feel sick.

But I also feel excited.

I begin typing.

[12]

WILL

I cook tea as soon as I'm home.

I say I cook tea — I put pie and chips in the oven and boil some tinned carrots.

I call Harper and she joins me at the table, staring at her phone. Even when I place her tea in front of her, she does not put it down.

Natalie joins us. She looks pale. She's thirty-eight, same as me, but you would think she was over fifty. Her hair is matted and, from the smell of her pyjamas, I'm pretty sure she's only just gotten out of bed.

She sits opposite Harper and pours the wine I didn't even realise she'd brought to the table.

"Are you sure—" I go to say, but the look she gives me shuts me up.

She drinks a few large gulps of wine then devours the pie. I prod at my chips, not feeling too hungry, and notice Harper hasn't touched hers yet; she is still on her phone.

"Honey, could you put that away while we're at the table?"

She ignores me. I stay calm.

"Honey?"

She still ignores me. I feel rage firing through me.

"Harper?"

When she ignores me again, I slam my fist on the table.

Natalie laughs.

And I know I'm pathetic. The only time I can show my anger and act like I'm in charge is with my daughter, and even then, I'm undermined by my wife.

"Harper, could you—"

"Oh, just let her," Natalie says. "If I had a phone when I was her age, I'd be texting all the boys too."

Harper glances at Natalie, and I see the disappointment in her face as she watches her mother drink her wine like it was juice. I want to save Harper from this, I want to show her that this isn't what family is, and that it's not how it should be.

But I can't.

I'm helpless. Even if I had the guts to tell my wife to leave, I'd let her back as soon as she barged through the front door drunk later that night.

And Harper would be a child of divorce, just like I was. Resenting her father for breaking up her family when she sees him every weekend.

No, I am doing everything I can to hold this family together.

"I just feel," I say cautiously, "that when we're at the table—"

"What?" Natalie barks. "We're going to talk? Share stories about our day?"

She laughs as she chokes on a mouthful of chips. She leaves the carrots.

"It's polite," I say.

She laughs again, her chuckles mixed with a cough.

Harper looks back at her phone and, in a way, maybe it's better she's on her phone. That way she doesn't have to look at what her home's become.

"Are you going out again tonight?" I ask Natalie as I take a polite spoonful of carrots on my fork.

"Probably."

"Could I be excused?" Harper asks, suddenly.

"Why?"

"I just..."

She doesn't say it, but I know what she wants to say.

She doesn't want to sit there and hear more about her mother's plans to get wasted.

She doesn't want to sit and hear her father speak like a pathetic, scared little boy to his own wife.

She doesn't want to be in this family.

And I wish there was a way to make her love me. Like she did when she was little. Like she did before she learned I'm a screw up.

"Yes," Natalie says, breaking the silence, and Harper gets up before I can object.

"Don't forget your tea," I say, but she leaves it, engrossed in her phone, and she stomps upstairs.

I drop my head. Close my eyes. Pretend this isn't how things are.

"What?" Natalie grunts.

I look up at her. She's staring at me and her eyelids are drooping and her eyes are bloodshot.

"Why?" I say, barely audible.

"What?"

"I just... What did I do?"

"What? You didn't do nothing."

She shoves the last few bites of her tea in her mouth and pours herself another glass of wine.

"Why don't you stay in tonight? We can have a nice night in. Watch a movie."

"Don't want to watch a movie."

"Then we can—"

"I said I don't want to watch a fucking movie."

She gets up, goes upstairs and comes down minutes later in a short dress.

I don't bother to object as she leaves.

And I'm left alone. Sat at the head of the table.

I clear away the plates and wash up. When I'm done, I go to bed. I'm tired.

I'm always so tired.

[13]

HARPER

I LIE UPSIDE DOWN ON MY BED, FEELING FLUTTERS OF excitement send tingles up and down my body.

It turns out he likes all the stuff that I like.

His favourite band is Paramore, his favourite movie is *Lord of the Rings,* and he says that, once he gathers the courage, he's going to get a tattoo of The Eye of Mordor on his bicep.

He says he's been on the message board for a few years as well and, even though I don't remember seeing his username before, it's pretty awesome.

What's more, he actually seems to care. When I send him a message, he's so eager to talk. I even sent him some poetry I wrote and he said he loves it.

You don't have to say that.

I'm not.

I mean, I know I'm not Carol Ann Duffy or Rupi Kaur.

Please, if only Duffy was as good as you!

Now I KNOW you're lying! Lol

I don't lie.

Everyone lies.

Everyone you've met lies.
You haven't met me.
Not yet, anyway.

Not yet?

Someday.

And what would we do if we did meet?

Go to the beach.
Have fish and chips.
Avoid the seagulls and stare at the sea.
You could read me more poetry.

Please, it's not that good!

I love it.
Like how you open with that line 'Sometimes I have a
memory and I'm not sure if it was a dream or reality.'
I TOTALLY know what you mean, that happens to me all
the time.

Seriously?

And you know what?

I don't care.

Reality be damned.

That could be the name of my poetry book.

Haha! YES!

He writes *haha*. Not *lol*.

Never *lol*.

He's too sophisticated for that.

Kids write *lol*. He isn't a kid. I mean, he's seventeen, but he's a grown up seventeen. Not the kind who spend all day on their Xbox, but the kind that spends all day reading, or watching foreign films, or going to gigs.

God, am I making up his personality now?

But what if I am! He was right when he said *reality be damned!*

Then he types something that makes me feel tense. Scared. Like this is all one sided.

Hey, we've been private messaging on this site quite

a bit.

I'm not sure if I like it.

I don't reply.

He doesn't like it?

What does he mean?

Can I have your number to iMessage you instead?

I breathe out a huge sigh of relief.

He just wanted my number.

God, I panicked.
I reply:

Of course :)

And I smile.
And I give it to him.

[14]
WILL

WE GO THROUGH ANOTHER PREVIOUS EXAM PAPER IN today's lesson. My students' attention wanders to the window or the door or, in some cases, a gormless stare at their pencil case.

One student stares at their crotch. I know they're on their phone; I'm not an idiot. But, you know what — they are doing it subtly. I can pretend I don't notice. I can ignore it and not have to create a meaningless confrontation.

The only person who seems to be paying attention is Destiny. She is transfixed, an adamant gaze following my every move. She doesn't look down at her exam paper once, she just stares at me. I can see her short skirt under the desk. She leaves her legs wide open. I don't know if she does this out of immature naivete, and that she doesn't know she is displaying her underwear to me — or whether she is doing it intentionally, purposefully, with complete knowledge of what she is doing. Either way, I do everything I can to avoid looking toward that area of the classroom. I sit on the desk and face the other way, or keep my head buried in the test paper I talk through, or aim my eyes at the ceiling, terrified that she may misinterpret my noticing as appreciation rather than horror.

Someone needs to tell her that it's inappropriate. That person, however, is not going to be me. Just imagine the accusations that could get thrown my way if I have a conversation with a girl about how her knickers are on display under the table. I'd be persecuted just for noticing what is impossible not to notice.

The best decision I could make is to ignore it.

The bell goes after a very long hour, and the students shuffle out for lunchtime.

Destiny does not.

She lingers behind, waiting for everyone else to leave, pausing as a straggler finally finishes packing his bag and goes.

She saunters to my desk and I immediately check that my classroom door is still open.

She stands there, smirking at me, a sultry smirk like the kind Natalie once used on me.

I look again to the open door, wishing she would use it.

"Hi, sir," she says. "Thanks for the great lesson again."

"No worries, Destiny."

She doesn't leave. She just stands there. Still staring at me.

"Can I help you with anything?" I ask.

"I was wondering if we could meet after school one day? I'm a bit worried about how I'm doing, and the exams are in a few months so it'd be really great if you could help me."

I would normally say yes, but in this situation, I am going to do everything I can to avoid this happening.

"I'm not sure I can accommodate that, I'm afraid, but I

do know Mrs Jennings does a revision class after school, she's two doors down."

"But I don't know Mrs Jennings. I was hoping it would be you, sir."

"I'm afraid not. But, again, I can recommend some tutors if—"

"Oh, I forgot!"

She puts her bag down — a red handbag with a bow on it — and reaches inside. She pulls out a box of chocolates, expensive ones, not the kind that you'd buy from a supermarket, but that you might order from *Thorntons*.

"I bought you these," she says, holding the box out, beaming at me.

I do not reach out to take them. In fact, I ensure that my hands go nowhere near them.

"That's really kind of you, Destiny, but I'm afraid I can't."

"Of course you can, sir. I got them to say thank you for being such a great teacher."

"Really, there is no need."

"Please, sir, I bought them especially."

"That really is very kind of you, but I'm not in the habit of accepting gifts from students."

"But I'm not just any student."

I wonder what she means by this but, before I can ruminate too much, she places the box on the keyboard of my laptop; somewhere I cannot help but touch them.

"I'll just leave them here, then."

"Please, I really don't think it's appropriate," I say, lifting the box and handing them back.

She puts her hands in the air and backs away.

"I'll see you later, sir," she says, and reverses out of the classroom, gives me one last lingering stare, then walks away.

I am sat here, holding a box of chocolates I determinedly did not want to be holding.

[15]

HARPER

I sit alone in the canteen, but I don't feel alone. I'm at an empty table, but it feels like Danny is right beside me.

Even when the girls laugh and make comments I don't listen.

Because I have something they don't.

Those boys that hang around their table and show off are only interested in their short skirts and faces plastered in make-up.

Danny is interested in so much more.

So what you up to now?

Oh, just at school. At lunch.

I'm not stopping you from being sociable, am I?
Don't want to take you away from your friends!

I pause. Consider what to say. Whether to lie, and say they don't mind and they are understanding and I've already spoken to them enough already.

But then I think... why lie? Why not just be honest? Why do I need to be anything but who I am?

I don't really have much in the way of friends.

Really?
That surprises me.

Why?

You just seem really nice.
I'd have thought you'd have lots of friends.

Afraid that's not the case.

I feel a bit uncomfortable. I change the conversation.

Do you have any siblings?

Nope. Only child.
You?

Same.

Parents divorced five years ago.
Not really too miserable about it.
Things are a lot better now I'm not having to drown out
their shouting with music.

My parents aren't divorced.
They probably should be.

How come?

I don't know if this is a conversation I want to get into.

Right now, he thinks I'm perfect. He likes who I am. If I tell him about my horrible homelife who knows if he'd still be interested?

But Danny is not like the other boys. He talks to me. He understands.

And it sounds like he's been through something pretty similar.

They barely talk.
I mean, they fight a lot, but then they stay silent for days,
and it's almost like I wish they would fight again.

I get what you mean.
It's like the silence is worse than the arguing.

Exactly

Like when they fight it's like they still actually care
enough to fight.
When they are silent, it's like they aren't even bothered
enough to shout at each other.
Like there's nothing left.

Wow. Totally.
How did you know all that?

I've been there.

Sounds like you really know what it's like.

Tell me about your dad.

My dad?
Why?

Just curious.

He's a loser.
Tries to talk to me like it makes up for being a shit
parent.
He lets my mum just walk all over him.

Perhaps he loves her.

What do you mean?

Perhaps he lets her get away with stuff because the
alternative is to let her go, and that's even worse.

I never thought of it that way.

Still, it is pretty pathetic.
He should still have some standards.

The bell goes for next lesson.

I want to stay here forever, in this seat, talking to Danny.

It's so easy.

I've got to go now.
Bell just went.

Talk later?

Of course.

And hey — who cares if you haven't got a load of friends to sit with?
You can always sit with me.

:)

I think everyone else is an idiot.
And you sound pretty special.

I smile.

Some of the girls look at me and frown, but I don't care.

They will not remove this smile from my face. I'm happy and their stupid frowns will do nothing about it.

He thinks I'm special.

I add:

You're pretty special too.

Then I put my phone in my pocket and go to English, unable to stop thinking about what I might say to him when we message later.

[16]

WILL

I have a free period last lesson, so I use it to mark books, and try not to get too irritated with the stupid answers I read.

It's like these kids learn nothing. Either they are stupid, or they are trying to annoy me.

For the question *How do we know x=5 in the equation?* a student has written: *Because sir told me.*

I lean back. Run my hands through my hair. Put the radio on. Something to distract me. A nice dose of radio 4 to keep me feeling calm.

I mark the next few books and check my emails as the news comes on.

"Hartbury College has released a statement regarding the teacher Patrick Armidge who was accused of misconduct by a female student on Friday, stating that the girl has since admitted she made the accusation up because she thought 'it would be funny.'"

I can't help but tut. How ridiculous. That girl has no idea what she's done to that man's life.

"Patrick Armidge has also released a statement saying

that, despite his suspension being lifted, he will not be returning to work as a teacher. Despite the allegations being false, he has stated that the physical abuse, mental abuse, media attention, and the damage it has done to his marriage is undoable, and that he does not wish to return to a career where he was treated as such despite being innocent."

I shake my head. I hope that girl feels ashamed of herself. I hope that she realises what she's done to a man just trying to earn a living and support his family.

Lost in thought, I reach for my coffee and knock it over, spilling the contents over the desk and over the box of chocolates bought for me by Destiny.

"Dammit," I mutter, and lift the box before wiping the rest of the table with a tissue.

Once I'm done, I go to wipe down the box and return it to the table, but it's pointless. The box is covered, it's ruined. And I didn't want it anyway.

I chuck it in the bin and forget about it.

I go to resume marking but I am sick of it. I was sick of it half an hour ago, now I am repulsed by it. The idea of picking up my red pen and writing another moan in another student's book just makes me want to pull my teeth out.

I stand. Walk around the classroom. Between the tables, stretching my legs. A glance out the window reveals a few students truanting their lessons on the football pitch, wrestling each other and laughing about it. I grow suddenly angry about how they are wasting their lives.

I used to ask kids, "Do you want to have a lot of money?"

They'd look bemused, and I'd prompt them again, and they'd reluctantly say, "Yes."

"Then work hard in school. The better qualifications, the better the job, the better the money."

Then I'd add, "I'm trying to help you be a millionaire here," although they never seem to find it amusing.

They would almost always quote the name of a famous person who has managed to be hugely successful without the benefit of education, and I'd be ready with my reply that they are the anomaly. The odds were far more in their favour if they left school with a few grades.

Now I don't bother asking them that. If they want to waste their opportunities then go for it. What does it matter to me?

With a sigh, I force myself out of my classroom and meander down the corridor. I need to get out of that room. I spend my life in there, battering knowledge into kid's heads, insisting they think creatively as they sit in rows and columns that are so rigidly set in their symmetry that I don't know how anyone could ever be creative in a room setup in such a uniformed way.

I sometimes look into classrooms and see the odd teacher who has their tables set out in a different way, at angles or grouped together or in one long row around the room. It sounds like a great idea, but that's just inviting students to screw around. I'm better off with the conformity that forces my students to become dull, mindless zombies.

I go to the staff room and approach the coffee machine, finding my mug in the sink with stains inside that indicates someone else has used it. I wash it up, pour the coffee in, then open the fridge to find there is no milk.

In fact, the only milk I can find is powdered milk in the cupboard. I try it, but it tastes disgusting, so I disregard the coffee, return my mug to the sink, and head back to my classroom just as the bell for the end of the day goes and doors open and students burst into the corridor, hurrying faster than they do at any other point of the day. Nothing wakes them up quite like the end of school.

Numerous children barge into me as they run past, but I ignore it. It's the end of the day. Let's just finish my work and go home.

When I return to my classroom, I don't even notice Destiny at first. She is crouched down, on her knees, her face in her hands, and I can't tell what she's doing.

"Destiny?" I say.

Her head shakes. She is still covering her face.

She is hunched over the bin.

What is she doing?

"Destiny, I really think you—"

"What's this?"

She lifts the coffee-stained box of chocolates from the bin.

"Oh, Destiny, I—"

"Do you know how much I spent on this? Not to mention the bus fayre to get into town and buy them for you?"

"Look, I—"

"Why would you do this?"

I go to speak, but don't. I look around the room, searching for the words.

"I think you need to go," I finally say.

She looks dumbfounded, shocked, bemused at the impudence of my reaction.

"I'm not going anywhere until you tell me why you did this!"

"I spilt coffee on them, Destiny, it was an accident."

"An accident?"

"Yes, an accident, I'm sorry."

I stay by the open door, glancing down the corridor, but there is no one there to help me.

She edges toward me, and it occurs to me that I am blocking her exit, so I walk in, moving behind the tables to keep the furniture between me and her.

She walks to the door and I think she's leaving — that is, until she shuts it.

"Destiny, please open the door," I say.

She stays in front of it. Slowly rotates toward me. Long strands of hair fall over her face, and she looks strange, disturbed, unhinged, and I want to do anything I can to get out of this situation.

"Hey, why don't we go to the staff room and get some towels. Maybe we could dry it off."

She shakes her head.

"Either way, just open the door, Destiny. Please. Just open it."

She licks her lips.

"Open the door!"

"I'm not that easy to get rid of, Will."

"It's Mr Coady, Destiny."

"That's what your other students call you."

"Exactly."

"I'm not like other students, am I?"

What do I do?

How do I get myself out of this situation?

I am scared. Not of her, but of what could happen if I don't deal with this properly.

"It's late," I say. "After school. How about you go home, and I go home, and we can talk about this later, right?"

Her fingers grip the box of chocolates, harder and harder, twisting it and capsizing it and destroying it.

She throws it in the bin.

"I know you'll realise the truth," she says.

"What? What truth?"

"I know you'll figure it out."

"Destiny, I—"

She leaves before I can finish my sentence, opening the door, backing into the corridor, then walking away.

I breathe a sigh of relief, then pack up my stuff and leave before she comes back.

[17]

HARPER

When I arrive home, I expect to find what I normally find. A silent home and bottles in the sink.

What I don't expect to find is a suitcase and Mum putting on a coat.

"Mum?" I say. "What's going on?"

She smiles at me in that condescending way adults do when they think I'm too young to understand — but I understand all too much. I would be annoyed, but this is the first time I've looked at her in the light for a while, and she doesn't look like the woman in the photo frames on the fireplace anymore. Her skin is wrapped tightly around her bones and her face is thin.

She looks ill, and not the kind you can make better.

"Oh darling," she says, looking at me as if she cares, and tilts her head to the side. Her voice is croaky. Her eyelids lull. Her breath wheezes.

"I don't understand," I say.

Right at that point, the front door opens, and I hate that today is the day Dad chooses to come home early from work. He could have found a note, instead he finds his wife on her way out.

Mostly, I hate how he doesn't even look surprised.

"What's going on?" he asks.

"I'm going to stay with my friend."

"What, Jane?"

"No, Will. A male friend."

I see how much its crushes Dad to hear this, I can see it on his face, the despair — but still no shock.

I wait for him to argue. For him to fight, tell her she's not going, say he'll take care of her like he always does, insist that they talk things through and work it out or even offer to pay for rehab again.

But he says nothing.

It is now the bastard chooses to say nothing.

"Dad..." I say, in an almost whisper, and I don't know why it's bothering me so much. It's not like they are a great couple together, and it's hardly like I'll miss out on any days we spend as a family — those days are long gone.

I just know that I don't want her to go.

Mum takes her suitcase and walks to the door. She pauses, looks at her husband, and he moves out of her way.

He moves out her way.

He moves. Out. Of. Her. Way.

He doesn't stop her, doesn't put his hand out to obstruct her or anything — he just lets her go.

And, within seconds, she is out of the door and into the darkness and gone from our lives.

Dad closes the door behind him. He doesn't look at me.

"What is wrong with you?" I say.

He still doesn't look at me. He doesn't even look up. He looks at his feet, like he's ashamed.

You're a grown man for fuck's sake, talk to your daughter.

"Why didn't you fight for her?" I ask.

He doesn't respond.

"Look at me!" I shout, and I feel my voice break under the strain of a scream I wasn't expecting.

He finally lifts his head to look at me, but he can't focus on my eyes. After a fleeting glance, he walks into the kitchen, muttering something like "I'll make us some fish and chips."

"Dad, stop it!"

He pauses in the doorway.

"I am your daughter — why won't you talk to me?"

I can see it's painful. I can see he's doing everything he can to avoid thinking about what's happened, to try not to cry in front of me.

I can't help it.

I'm mad. I'm enraged. I'm furious.

I don't know why; I wanted this. I wanted them apart so they could be the parents they could possibly be without the other one in the way — but, seeing Dad now, wandering aimlessly into the kitchen like he's lost a pet, I know that it won't improve anything.

What is Dad's purpose now without Mum to take care of?

"Dad, please, just go get her. Tell her to come back. Tell her — I don't know, just... Tell her something."

"I don't know what to tell her." His voice is quiet, like it's hidden away in the shadows. He hasn't even switched the kitchen light on.

"You are pathetic. Do you know that?"

He doesn't reply.

He doesn't need to.

I charge upstairs, shut my door, and refuse to answer it to anyone. I swear, if anyone comes in, I will scream at them, but secretly, I hope that Dad will knock on that door, and that he will hug me and tell me everything will be okay.

He doesn't.

[18]

WILL

I can't say I wasn't expecting it, but that doesn't make it any less shocking.

The worst part? That I don't even have the energy to be jealous. She's going to another man's house. She's leaving me for him, whoever he is. Probably another drunk, someone who will encourage her habit rather than try to help her — and I can't even muster the energy to hate her.

Harper wants to see more from me. More vigour. More umph.

I know she does.

But I have nothing left. I'm drained. I'm soulless. I gave everything to this marriage, everything to my career, everything to being a father, and I am left with nothing but broken pieces of a home, and a wife and daughter who hate me.

I consider going upstairs. Knocking on Harper's door. Speaking to her.

But what would I say?

Sorry I'm so gutless, I'll do better?

She's right to be angry, and I don't know how I'm supposed to quell it.

I wonder how this will affect her when she's older, and I hate myself even more. I'm supposed to be her role model. Me and Natalie are meant to be the example of what a happy marriage looks like.

All we've done is isolate her from us.

I find one of Natalie's half-finished bottles of wine on the shelf. I fill a glass and drink it.

Without realising it, I remove my phone from my pocket, unlock it, and hover my thumb over Natalie's number.

Should I just give her a bit of time? Talk about things once she's calmed down?

Another glass of wine removes my inhibitions, and I call her, listening to the rings until they take me to voicemail.

What do I do with my evening now?

Watch a television show that doesn't matter? Go to sleep early? Mark books and plan lessons?

Is that all there is to my life?

Or I could just sit and sulk in the darkness, keep ringing her, and wait until my legs choose to carry me to bed.

[19]
HARPER

THE FIRST THING I DO IS TEXT DANNY. I'VE NEVER HAD
that before, having someone to go to — I've dealt with every
problem I've ever had on my own.

Not anymore.

My mum left.

He replies within a minute.

Are you serious?

Yep. I came home and she had a suitcase.

Is your dad okay?

He came home just after me and saw it.

Didn't even do anything.
Didn't even put up a fight.

Oh my god, I'm so sorry.

I just can't believe he didn't even bother.
What kind of a man doesn't care about his wife leaving?
He didn't even cry.

Maybe he was trying to be strong.
For you, I mean.

My dad doesn't care enough to be strong.
There's nothing 'strong' about him.
He's weak.

Maybe it was for the best.

Maybe.
Still sucks though.
I mean, mother of your daughter walks out for another
man and you don't even care?

Shit.
Another man?

Yep.

Do you know who he is?

Don't know. Don't care.

This is really shit, I'm sorry to hear it.

Is there anything I can do?
Would you like me to send you a picture?
Of me, I mean.

I consider this question, lying upside down on my bed, staring at the ceiling as guitars blare out my speakers.

I wish there was something he could do.

Some way to make me feel better.

Yes please!
Send me a picture.
One of you smiling.
One that will make me happy.

He doesn't reply, and I worry I was too demanding, but after a minute one comes through.

I can't quite believe what I'm seeing.

He's so handsome.

Ruffled hair, chiselled chin, clear skin.

Your turn.

God, no. He's too good for me. He's too out of my league, I don't want him to see what I look like.

I panic.

But he's not like that. I'm sure of it. I trust him. He trusts me. I know who he is.

I turn the camera round and take a selfie. The first few look stupid, but I finally find one that looks the least stupid, and I send it.

Wow.
You're gorgeous.

No I'm not.

You really are.
I was worried you were going to secretly be a fifty-year-old man or something.

I chuckle.

Then another picture comes through.

In this one, he's topless. Slim. Athletic.

Wow, you really are hot.

Your turn.

What do you mean?

I sent a picture of me without my top on...

It takes a moment for me to understand what he's saying, and then...

Oh, God, I don't know if I want to do that. I feel nervous.

But good nervous, I guess. Excited.

No one's ever seen me without a top on — no one outside the girl's changing rooms after PE, that is, and even then I tend to face the wall.

But he sent me one...

I guess I probably should.

> *No pressure.*
> *Just want to see : P*

I take off my top. Look at my belly. If I breathe in, I can make it flat. If I take the photo from a high angle my breasts might even block it out.

I'm wearing a purple bra. I've never really thought about what bra I'm wearing before. I've never had to.

I take the picture and send it before I can convince myself not to.

> *:P :P :P :P ;) ;) ;) ;)*
> *Wow.*
> *I am lucky to be talking to someone so stunning.*

Please, I am not stunning.

> *You really don't know, do you?*

Don't know what?

Just how beautiful you are.

I'm not beautiful.

I wish your dad could see what I see.
If he realised what an amazing girl you are, perhaps he'd
treat you like an adult.

A sting of sadness hits me.

I'd been smiling so much, he'd been making me feel so good, and now...

He seems to realise this, as after a few minutes silence he sends another message.

Sorry, I shouldn't have said that.
I didn't mean to bring your dad up again.
I mean, I meant what I said, I just hope I haven't
upset you.

You haven't upset me.

Are you sure?

Yeah.
I don't know.
It sucks that my dad doesn't even care enough to talk
to me.

It does. That's not what a real dad is like.

I guess.

He deserves to be hurt.

That's a bit harsh.

Don't you think he does?
He causes you so much pain, doesn't he deserve any?

I suppose.
When you put it like that.

I just hate guys like him.
I'm sorry if that's too forthright.

It's okay.
I'm just really glad I have you to talk to.

And I am.

And now I have two pictures of him.

Two pictures that I gaze at all night before falling asleep with my phone in my hand.

[20]

WILL

I DON'T GET MUCH SLEEP. AND I DON'T EVEN remember eating breakfast.

I'm sure I ate it, but I don't remember it. I feel like I was a puppet, or being controlled by a parasite. I walked through my house, drove to work, listened to the radio, and tried calling Natalie a few times, and remember none of it.

It isn't until now, when I am sat at the desk of my decrepit classroom, looking at sparse posters with torn corners and cracked cream walls and tables with gum stuck under them that I think — what the hell am I doing?

Am I getting a divorce?

Am I living on my own?

Am I going to be a single parent?

Natalie didn't seem bothered about fighting for custody of Harper, but who knows if that will change. Plus, Harper's old enough to decide where she stays. Why would she choose me?

I bow my head. Run my hands through my hair.

I try calling Natalie again. I have ten minutes. But, after trying three times and receiving no answer, I stop, distracted by thoughts of Harper. We are about to heap so much childhood trauma on her and there's nothing I can do about it. Watching her mum walk out and her dad breakdown and her parents separate is going to affect her in so many ways. She will probably discuss this experience in therapy someday, she will end relationships because of intimacy issues caused by us, and she will resent me until the day she dies...

And I hate myself for it.

I hate myself so much.

I'm a useless teacher. Useless husband. Useless man. But I really don't want to be a useless father — yet I have no idea what to do to save Harper from the inevitable pain.

Either way, I've got to stop thinking about it. I have a day full of lessons to get through. I have hours of monotony to force upon disinterested adolescents.

God, I'd have hated me as a student. I'd have dreaded my lessons. I'd have taken the piss out of me and wondered if I had a life.

I open my laptop and the screen comes to life, though it will still take another ten minutes to load. On the keyboard is an envelope, one that had been wedged inside my closed laptop, and the front reads *Mr Coady*. It is written with childish, curly writing, and with hearts scribbled decoratively around it.

My immediate thought is Destiny.

I consider whether to open it. I dread what I'm going to find.

But I have to open it.

Otherwise I'll have no idea what I'm dealing with.

I turn the envelope over to find that it has been sealed with a kiss — literally, the imprint of lipstick marks the seal.

I close my eyes and shake my head. I could just take this straight to the Headmaster.

But I've already given him enough ammunition. He already hates me enough — can I really trust him not to misinterpret the situation? I don't even need to be guilty — just the accusation alone would be enough to ruin me; look what happened to Patrick Armidge.

I open the envelope, worried about what I might find — but it's just a letter.

The first line starts *Dear Will.*

While she addressed the envelope to me as Mr Coady, she is now addressing the letter to my first name.

And I'm scared.

For the first time in this situation, I am not just worried or annoyed, I am fearful for both my career, and my freedom.

Reluctantly, I read the letter.

Dear Will,

I want to say sorry for my reaction yesterday. I understand it would have been an accident for you to spill your coffee on the chocolates. If you'd like, I can go and get some more for you after school. I really don't mind.

I also want to say how happy I am to have you in my life. It's taken a while for us to get to know each other, but love grows over time, and we've got plenty of time. With each passing day, our affection grows stronger, and I know I mean as much to you as you mean to me.

It is such a cliché to say that you'd die for someone. I've always seen it in romance movies and scoffed, thinking it's just so Romeo and Juliet. But now I finally see what they mean.

Because I would, Will.

I would die for you.

When you meet your soul mate, you know — and I know, just like you do, that we are destined to be together.

Our love is special, unlike any other, and they won't understand — but they don't need to.
I will always be yours, whether we keep it a secret or shout it from the rooftops.

Forever and always your girl,
Destiny
X X X X X X X X

I hold the letter in my hands. Re-read it.

It's shaking.

I don't realise at first, but that's because my arms are shaking.

Fuck.

I mean...

Fuck.

This isn't just someone who has a crush on their teacher, or has an infatuation — she seems to believe her affections are reciprocated.

She seems convinced that this is a two-way thing.

And I don't know what to do.

Should I report it?

Of course I know I should report it, but it's not that simple, is it?

I open Google. I type in the name of the teacher I'd heard the news reports about — Patrick Armidge.

Straight away, the top results are news websites with headlines such as:

Teacher Falsely Accused Goes Into Hiding.

Falsely Suspected Teacher Physically Attacked By Parents.

Disgraced Former Teacher's Wife: "I Want a Divorce."

This man was innocent. The girl admitted it. It was a lie. But look at what a false accusation has done to him...

His life is over. He's been attacked on all fronts.

I wouldn't care. My marriage is over, my life is shit anyway — but what about Harper?

Could I put Harper through that?

She's disappointed enough in me, I know she is — but if she believed I was doing something with a student, how much more would she hate me?

God, what if I lost her...

What if she was taken away...

What if she was attacked because of association...

I know I should report it, but even a false allegation, some sort of retaliation for my reporting it, would be enough to destroy my daughter's life.

I can't make things any worse for her.

I'll talk to Destiny. I will. I'll talk to her properly, and make it clear that this is not okay, that there is no love there.

That's what I'll do.

I'm not sure if it will work, but it's the next step, it's what I will try next.

Destiny is unstable. Perhaps we'll understand each other. Two messed-up people with broken hearts.

I just hope it works.

I do.

I really do.

[21]

HARPER

Lunchtime arrives and I'm still thinking about last night.

Normally my parent's marriage doesn't bother me for this long. Maybe it did when I was little, but I've become so used to it that it's rarely more than a mild irritation. Like the fleeting annoyance I get when a teacher sets homework or the router needs resetting — it's just part of life.

This feels different.

Mum left. She actually left. She's never done that before. She's threatened it, quite a lot actually, but she's never packed a bag and she's never walked through that door without returning later that night.

Dad was like a zombie this morning. He didn't even ask me if I wanted a lift, or wish me a good day. He looked like he hadn't slept. In a way, I miss his annoying morning talk. It doesn't feel right that he doesn't try and talk to me while I eat my breakfast.

At first, this made me think of him as human. As someone who's suffering. As someone in pain, and that maybe I should cut him some slack.

Then I remembered what Danny said.

He's not what a real dad is like.

It's true. A real dad would fight to stop his wife leaving, would do anything he could to stop his family from breaking apart.

But he didn't even bother.

As I sit alone at my table, prodding a dry piece of bread, my phone buzzes. It's Danny, and that forces a little bit of a smile.

> *Hey.*
> *You okay?*
> *Sorry if I was a bit too full-on last night.*

> *What do you mean?*

> *When I said your dad deserves to be hurt.*

I think about this for a while.

I could have taken offence to that; I could have found it a bit weird. But I didn't.

In fact, I was pleased that someone said it.

That someone was able to voice an opinion I would be ridiculed for.

> *It's okay.*
> *You're probably right.*

> *How you doing today?*

Dunno.
Not great I guess.
Glad I have you to talk to though :)

Aw me too.
I just want to help in some way.

It feels strange that someone wants to help me. No one's ever helped me. No one's ever cared that much.

Want to beat up my dad for me? lol

I regret putting *lol*. He's too grown up for that.

And now I think about it, I regret the joke. It was a bit morbid.

Still, he doesn't seem to mind.

Oh, yeah, sure.
Just name the time and date and I'll fetch my cricket
bal.

He makes me chuckle at least. Silly as it is.

Cricket bat?

Didn't take you for a cricketer.

Well, I'm full of surprises.

Maybe it's not the best idea.
Wouldn't want to damage your cricket bat.

It's seen better days anyway.
Maybe you'll have to beat him up instead.

HAH! Yeah sure.
Do you know what tho…
Don't even think he'd be bothered if I did.
He'd probably just sit there and take it.
That's how little he cares.

And how would you do it?

Dunno.
I don't own a cricket bat!

Haha.
Seriously.
*If you were going to hurt your dad, how would you
hurt him?*

The question throws me.

It's strange.

I wasn't expecting it, and it's not something I'd really thought about.

Of course, I've shouted at him and told him to leave me

alone and told him he's useless — but that was more frustration than with intention to hurt him.

Not sure.

Think about it.
What would you do?

I think psychological torture would be best.
He's a teacher — maybe I could plant dodgy pictures on his laptop or something.

Haha!
You are evil.

Or I could do it while he's sleeping.

Do what?

Do what?
What is it I'm even talking about?
What am I suggesting?

Dunno.
Not sure where I'm going with this tbh.
It's hardly like I will do anything.

What if you had to kill someone?

What?

If you had to kill someone, how would you do it?

If I had to kill someone?

Yeah.
Like, would you burn them to death, or would you bury
them alive?

I'm not sure how to take this.

I can't see his face so I can't see his expression. I don't know if he's smiling while he says this, or whether he's grimacing.

A few seconds go by as I try and think of what to reply, and he sends me a message.

Sorry.
That was quite a horrific question to ask out of context.
I was joking.

Ok.

It's something me and my mates joke about sometimes.
Like, how we would get rid of our least favourite
teacher.
(It's Mr Jennings btw — he teaches Geography and
always has wet pits.)

It's all right, he was joking. It's hard to tell sometimes when you're messaging.

That's okay.
I don't really have any friends, so I don't really know
what friends joke about.

I'm your friend.

I know you are.

I'm more than your friend.
If that's what you want me to be, that is.

Of course.

:)

:)

[22]

WILL

IT'S AFTER SCHOOL AND, ALTHOUGH I HAVEN'T ASKED
to see Destiny, she turns up. Smiling, fiddling with her hair,
biting her bottom lip, her skirt hiked up. I was in the midst
of trying to call Natalie again, but her presence forces me to
put my phone down.

She bounces in and sits on the edge of the desk, and her
skirt rides up her legs even further, and it's so inappropriate
that I can't believe none of the female teachers have had a
conversation with her about this.

"Hey, Will," she says.

"It's Mr Coady," I say, turning to face her. "Or sir."

She giggles playfully.

"Sorry, sir." The way she says sir is slow and deep, and
she almost sounds like a real woman.

I pick up the letter and place it on the desk.

"What's this?" I ask.

"Oh, you found it!"

"Of course I found it, Destiny, you left it on my laptop."

"I'm just not that good at saying how I feel, so I thought
it best to write it down."

"Right, but…" I wish I'd thought through what I was going to say. "It's not really okay to send these letters to your teacher, is it?"

"Oh, I don't do it to any other teacher, don't worry. It's only you."

"But it's not appropriate."

"Why not?"

"You are my student, not my girlfriend."

Her eyes light up on the word *girlfriend,* and it's like she's ignored every other word of the sentence and focussed on just that one.

"I think you need help," I tell her. "Counselling, maybe. This isn't normal behaviour."

"What isn't normal behaviour?"

"This… Nonsense you wrote."

"Did I ramble?"

"No, Destiny, you aren't getting it — it is crazy."

She smiles again. Even blushes.

"Love like this is crazy, Will. That's what makes it so special."

"It's not love, Destiny, we are not in love!" I stop and take a moment to make sure I keep my voice down. "Why won't you listen to me?"

"I'm listening, I just don't think you know what you're saying."

"This has got to stop. Please. The chocolates, the letter… It could land me in trouble."

"I'm not going to tell anyone."

"That's not the point — even you saying these things to me, it makes me look bad."

"You don't look bad."

"No, you're not getting it!"

I stand. Clench my fist and raise it to my mouth, doing

all I can to remain calm. I wander back and forth, trying to think of what to say, aware of her eyes following me everywhere I go.

"Will?" she says, standing up.

"It's Mr Coady!"

"Oh, Will, stop it."

"Did you not just listen to me? I said not to call me Will. You are a student, and that's all you'll ever be."

"To everyone else."

"No, Destiny — to me."

Her smiles fades a little. Some of this seems to have gone through. Maybe she's even beginning to understand.

"I don't love you, Destiny. And it's not appropriate for you to say you love me."

She bows her head. Her hair falls over her face and I can't tell if she's crying. It sounds like she's sobbing, but when she lifts her head up and pulls her hair back, there are no tears there.

She gets up. Goes for the door. I think she's leaving, but she's not — she's closing it.

I rush after her, go to open the door, but before I know it, she has turned to me and wrapped her arms around my neck.

"Stop it!" I tell her. "Get off me!"

She moves onto her tiptoes and purses her lips and her arms bring my head closer to hers, so much so I can't get away, and I can do nothing to stop her lips meeting mine.

I try to push her off. I place my hands on her shoulders and use all my force, and she has such a tight grip, but finally I remove her and I back up, out of her reach.

She bites her lip. Smiles a smile only adults should use.

"See?" she says. "How can you say there's nothing there with a kiss like that?"

I shake my head. Keep backing away until I am as far from her as I can be. This was a stupid idea. I have no choice in what I should do next.

"I'm going to have to report this," I tell her. "I'm going to have to tell someone what you've done."

"What I've done? Don't you mean what we've done."

"You kissed me."

"I know."

"And I'm going to have to—"

"Will, please. You kissed me too. And if you start telling people that I kissed you, then I will tell them the truth."

"Truth? What truth?"

"That you love me. That you kissed me too."

"Destiny, please stop."

"I can't. I'm in too far."

I say nothing.

She says nothing.

We stare at each other, at opposite ends of the classroom.

She's right.

I can't say anything.

Not now. Not with how it will look.

"Please, just leave me alone," I say, and it comes out in a whimper.

She backs up to the door.

"You may want to wipe your lips," she tells me. "You've got my lip gloss on you."

I wipe my lips on the back of my hand and it leaves a smear of sparkles.

She lifts her hand and waves with her fingers, then reverses through the doorway and finally leaves.

And she's right. Of course she's right.

I didn't report her when she gave me chocolates. Or when she gave me the letter.

And if I was to report her now, it would look far, far worse.

[23]

HARPER

I walk home the long way, by the river. Thinking of Mum. Thinking of Dad.

Thinking of Danny.

If I had to kill someone, how would I do it?

What a question.

Is that what people joke about?

When I see those girls with their friends and the boys, are they making jokes about mortality and murder?

I open my phone. I have a message from Danny and I can't wait to read it, but first, I open my contacts and go to Mum's number.

I'm not sure why I've gone to this number.

Should I ring it?

And say what?

Mum hasn't said a word to me for a long time. Dad is useless, but he still tries to make conversation.

I click away from her number and open my messages.

What's on your mind, gorgeous?

He makes me smile. But he also makes me worried. If he met me, would he still think I'm gorgeous?

Not much.
Just lost in thought.

Parent troubles?

What else?

Bah, parent's be damned.
Think of me instead.
Hopefully that's a far more pleasant thought :)

I smile, and continue walking home, ignoring all those pesky thoughts that tell me I'm worthless and that my parents don't want me because there's something wrong with me.

Danny wants me even if they don't.

He can be my family now.

[24]

WILL

As I drive home, I'm buzzing with anger, and I do the only thing I can do to take my mind off all of this nonsense with Destiny — phone Natalie again. With my phone connected to Bluetooth speakers, I leave it unlocked as I drive and keep pressing her number, over and over, automatically — so automatic, in fact, that when she actually answers it takes me by surprise.

"Hello?"

She sounds tired.

"Natalie? Natalie, oh my God!"

"Will, you need to stop calling me."

"No, I know, just please — don't hang up, okay?"

"What do you want?"

That's a good question. In my persistence in trying to get through to her, I'd completely forgotten why I was trying to talk to her. What do I actually want to say?

"Can we — can we meet? And talk?"

"Will, I don't think there's much point."

"You're my wife, Natalie, I—"

"Will, we're separated, that doesn't mean much anymore."

"Look, Natalie, can't we just... I don't know. Meet. Discuss things."

"I don't think—"

I hear a man's voice. He sounds annoyed. It's muffled, but I'm sure he asks her something about whether it's me ringing again.

I recognise that voice.

"Who is that? Is that Brian? Are you at Brian's?"

Brian is an idiot who's spent the last five or so years telling Natalie I'm not good enough for her and that there's nothing wrong with her drinking. I used to call him a friend, now I only call him names.

"Right, don't go anywhere. I'm coming over."

"Will, please don't."

"I'll be there in ten minutes."

I hang up and look for somewhere to turn around. I use a junction to the left, and don't notice a car having to slam on their brakes because of me. Their horn and hand gesture make their feelings about me clear, but I ignore it; I'm protected in my car, and I have more important things to worry about.

It's been a few years since I've been to Brian's place. We used to have dinner with Brian and his wife until they split up and Brian became an alcoholic. He's a lecherous, predatory bloke, one that would sooner take advantage of a drunk girl than help her home, and I can't believe she's left me for *him*.

Has she been with him all this time, getting drunk and fucking before coming home to me so I can pick up the mess?

I pull up across the end of his drive and push myself

from the car. I catch my reflection in the window; my suit is ill-fitting, my tie flutters chaotically in the wind, and my hair sticks up in all the wrong places. I never realised quite how awful I look.

Right now I do not care.

I bang against the door with my fist, full of energy, full of fight. When Brian opens the door, looming over me in the doorway, my adrenaline is immediately replaced with fear.

"What the fuck do you want, Will?" he asks, walking out of his house toward me, forcing me to back up.

"I — I — I want to see my wife," I stutter.

"Well your wife doesn't want to see you."

"It's not up to you—"

"Get the fuck off my property before I break your neck, yeah?"

I want to run away. I feel myself cowering, I feel my eyes watering, my arms shaking — but isn't this the problem? That I'm such a coward all the time?

If ever there is an instance for me to find a modicum of courage, this is it.

Unfortunately, I can't find any, and I just keep backing away.

"You — you — you —"

"You what? Look at you. You're pathetic. You can't even stand straight."

"I—"

He grabs my collar.

"Brian," says a familiar voice from behind him.

Natalie's gentle hand rests on Brian's arm, and Brian releases me.

"Go back inside," Brian tells her. "I'm dealing with this."

"Let me talk to him," she says. "It's fine."

Brian looks back at her. It's been a long time since I've seen her in the daylight. She's pale and scarily thin, with bags under her eyes and veins sticking out of her arms.

Brian gives me a final glare and says, "You come back to my property again, I'll kill you," before walking back inside the house.

And here we are. Me and my wife. Standing face-to-face, just feet apart, as I'd been wanting. For the first time, I look at the woman I married, and have no idea what to say.

"You look awful," I tell her.

She tuts and sighs. It probably wasn't the best opening line.

"Please, just come home with me," I say. "We'll forget all about this. We'll get you some help."

She folds her arms. Shakes her head. Sighs and looks down, then looks back up at me.

"Natalie?"

"You do realise I've been sleeping with him, don't you?" she says, her voice soft and soothing. I expected aggression, but there is none — just resolve.

"What, Brian?"

"Yes."

"For how long?"

She shrugs. "Years."

"God, Natalie..."

"This day was going to happen. Eventually, I was going to leave. We both knew that."

"I didn't."

She smiles like one would smile to a naive child.

"We can work on it," I say. "I've not always been the best husband, I know that, I probably drove you away from me, I get it, but we can figure it out."

Natalie laughs, and it kills me.

"I tell you I've been cheating on you for years, and you beg me to come back to you? What is wrong with you, Will?"

"I don't care."

"But you should! If your wife cheats on you, you should care! It should make you angry, but I don't see it. Where is your anger, Will? Why don't you get angry with me?"

"You're an alcoholic. You don't know what you're doing."

"An alcoholic? I'm living the life I want to live."

"Just because you're unhappy."

"And you're not?"

"Not with you."

"What's the common denominator here, Will? What is it that's driving me to drink, and driving you to despair?"

I don't say anything. Not because I'm not bursting with things to respond with, but because none of MY responses will help the situation.

"I'm going back inside now," she tells me. "And I don't want you to bother me again. I'll talk to a divorce lawyer we'll get the process started."

She turns to go, but I pull her arm and turn her around. She hits my arm away from her.

"Sorry," I say.

"Go home, Will."

"But—"

"We don't love each other anymore."

"I do."

She shakes her head. "Well, I don't."

She turns to go back inside.

Then I remember — Harper. What about her? What about her daughter? What about the one thing that should matter?

"But what about—"

She turns around with a huff. Looks at me with such an intense weariness.

She doesn't seem interested. If I'm beginning to be honest with myself, she hasn't been interested in me or her daughter for quite some time.

"Nothing," I say. "Never mind."

She returns back inside.

I return to my car.

And as I drive home, trying to avoid people in other cars seeing me cry, I wonder when it was that she stopped loving me.

Was it yesterday? A year ago? Ten years ago?

Or did she ever love me at all?

[25]

HARPER

I hear Dad walk through into the house. He
stumbles and swears as he slams the door, finding some
minor inconvenience and blowing it up into a catastrophe.

I lay upside down on my bed with my feet on the wall.

Danny and I have been texting all evening, but he says
he's being called for tea and that he'll speak to me later, and
now I'm left with silence.

Not that there was any noise while we were texting,
except in my head, where there was a symphony of beautiful crescendos and elaborate melodies played by a glorious
orchestra.

I wasn't sure I believed love was a thing. Can you blame
me, with the parents I have? Dad would insist he loves
Mum, but if love is holding the hair of your wife back while
she throws up every night, then I'm not sure I want it.

Then again, maybe that wasn't love. Or it was their
version of love. Or it was habit.

Because what I'm feeling now is nothing like that. I
don't see a way it could be possible that Danny and I end up
in the routine of misery my parents' marriage spiralled into.

And it isn't that I don't believe love happens to people... I just never thought it happened to me.

But he says I'm special. That I deserve love, and I almost cried, which was strange, as I never thought it was something that would make me cry, the idea that I deserve love. Perhaps I never thought about it, or maybe I never let myself dwell on the notion of whether I was actually loveable.

Now I do. Because he thinks I am.

He says I am.

He *knows* I am.

I look at my phone screen. He's not texted back yet. How long can dinner take?

And that is when my thoughts are interrupted by a few knocks on the front door.

Who could that be?

We never get visitors.

Then I think — is it Mum? Is she back? Has she come to apologise?

I leap from my bed to the window, ignoring the head rush, hoping to see her suitcase on the driveway while she hugs Dad.

But I don't see a suitcase on the driveway.

I don't see Mum.

All I see is a police car.

[26]

WILL

The knock on the door is confident. Three definite strikes that echo around the house.

My first thought is that Natalie has changed her mind — but that is not Natalie's knock, and even so, she would just walk in.

Which makes me question who it is, and I stare at the door, trying to figure it out.

The knocks come again, breaking me out of my trance, and I open the door.

A police officer fills the frame, his white shirt sleeves beneath a stab proof vest. He's taller than I am, and a lot more muscular.

"Hi, are you Will Coady?" he asks, his voice deep and gruff.

I nod, unable to keep my mouth from hanging open.

My body stiffens.

Destiny.

She must have told someone something, and he's here to arrest me. My life will become like Patrick Armidge's. My daughter will disown me. Guilty or not, I'll forever be seen as a sex offender.

"May I come in?" he says.

"Er..."

No, I do not want you to come in, I am tempted to say. But I am not the kind of person to say that to a regular guy, never mind a police officer.

"Okay," I say, opening the door for him, then for some reason, I add, "would you like a cup of tea?"

"Oh, that would be great," he says. "Two sugars."

I'm confused.

If he's here to arrest me, then why is he having a cup of tea?

"Am I in trouble?" I ask as I walk into the kitchen, and I hate myself for the quiver I can hear in my own voice.

I put the kettle on. Get a cup. Put the teabag in. Add two sugars.

"You? No, not at all. I'm here to talk to you about your daughter, Harper."

Harper?

What has she done?

Nothing. Surely. She barely leaves the house. She wouldn't steal anything or hurt anybody. She hardly has any friends to be antisocial with. What could she have done?

"Is Harper in at all?"

"Yes, she's upstairs."

"Perhaps it would be a good idea if you were to ask her to come down. It would be good to speak to both of you."

"Has she done something?"

"She has not broken the law, no. But we are worried she may be in danger."

Seeing the look on my face, he adds, "Not any imminent danger, no need to worry. I just need to talk to her."

"Okay."

The kettle finishes boiling. I pour the water into the cup. Add some milk. Place it on the counter before the police officer. Then I go to the bottom of the stairs and call out Harper's name.

She doesn't come out of her room. Of course she doesn't.

I call again.

After no response, I tut and begin to make my way upstairs. That is when she opens her door.

"Dad..." she says. "Why is there a police car outside?"

"An officer is here. He wishes to talk to you. To us. Both of us."

"Why?"

"I don't know. Could you come down please?"

She looks away, a weak look in her eyes, and she looks so young.

"You're not in trouble, Harper, please just come down."

She shuts her door and makes her way slowly down the stairs, and we emerge into the kitchen together.

The police officer's stare lingers on Harper. He smiles a little, like he's looking at a niece he hasn't seen in a while.

"What's going on?" she asks, her voice small and timid.

"I will explain everything," he says. "Just please know, you are not in any trouble."

"Okay..."

"Is there somewhere we could sit?"

"Yeah," I reply. "In the living room. This way."

He smiles and follows us.

[27]

HARPER

ME AND DAD SIT ON THE EDGE OF THE SOFA, AND THE
police officer sits on the armchair opposite. He takes up the
whole seat, and I've never seen someone who looks so confident. He leans forward and smiles at me in a way that I
imagine is meant to be reassuring, but is not.

"I just realised I never introduced myself," he says.
"Forgive me. My name is Officer Simon Felix."

He offers his hand to me, and I shake it. His grip is firm
and makes my loose hand feel small in his.

He shakes Dad's hand too, who offers his in return just
as tentatively.

"Have you heard of a girl called Linda Salborough?" he
asks.

Dad shakes his head.

Yes, I have heard of her. I was abused for posting an RIP
for her on the message board.

I remain silent.

"She was a young woman, about your age." He indicates
me. "Who had quite a large presence on a message board
that I believe you post on."

Dad looks at me, confused, and I suddenly feel defensive. There's nothing wrong with going on message boards.

"You may not know this, but she was found a few weeks ago. Dead. In her bedroom. Following an overdose. It was believed to be suicide, and we had no reason to question that. Until now."

He looks from Dad to me, like he's trying to gauge our reactions, like he's looking for shock on our faces, and I wish he'd just get to the point.

"Upon closer examination of her computer, we found that she had taken a video of her suicide and streamed it live to another person's computer. We looked further into this, and found thousands of messages between her and this boy, both on her computer and on her phone. This was a boy that she met on the message boards."

He takes a moment. Takes a breath. Looks between us, then places his focus back on me, and chooses his next words carefully.

"This boy — if he is in fact a boy, as he may well not be who he said he was — convinced Linda to kill herself. And to film it. In order to join something called The Death Club — an exclusive club for people whose death has gone viral. Fortunately, we managed to find this video before it could be spread across the internet. Linda never got to join this club; not that she'd know."

"What is this got to do with Harper?" Dad asks.

"Well, Harper. Why don't you tell us? Have you been approached by anyone on the message board recently?"

He looks at me.

Dad looks at me.

Their stares are like daggers being fired at my skin.

Felix knows. Of course he knows. He's asking me questions he already has the answers to, and it annoys me that he's trying to play me — that he's trying to get me to tell him exactly what he wants to hear.

So I say nothing.

Dad looks from Felix to me.

Eventually, Felix breaks the silence.

"We know you've been speaking to a boy, Harper. We know he messaged you via the message boards, and we know that you've been texting on your phone."

Dad stares at me like I've done something awful, and I hate him even more in this moment. I have done nothing wrong. I met a boy, he likes me, and Dad can go to hell.

"So?" I say.

"This boy may not be who he says he is."

"How do you know that?"

"We don't know that yet—"

"Exactly."

Felix pauses, giving himself a moment to think about what to say.

"I know this isn't easy to hear," he says. "But we believe he may be the one who manipulated Linda into—"

"You believe?"

"Yes, we believe."

"So you don't *know*."

"Not yet."

"Then why are you saying these things?"

"Harper, I..." Dad interjects. "How could you be so foolish? To give your number to a boy you met online... You have no idea who he is."

"He sent me a picture."

"And how do you know that is a picture of him?"

My arms are shaking I'm so angry.

No, I'm beyond angry. I'm enraged.

Who the hell does he think he is?

He's never been a father before. Never bothered. What, now the police officer is here he's going to pretend to care?

It's all a show. Trying to look good. Trying to look like he's a parent, but he's not.

And I don't believe a word of it.

"I know this is tough to hear," Felix says.

"You don't know anything. He's nice to me."

"Harper, come on," Dad says, with increasing condescension. "Of course he's nice to you. That's how these predators get you. He'll be nice and get you to trust him."

"You should listen to your father," Felix says, and I direct my scowl at him.

"My father?" I say. "He's only pretending to care because you're here. Normally he doesn't give a shit."

"Harper!" Dad says. "Of course I care. You're my whole world."

I scoff.

"You barely talk to me. You never try."

"You make it pretty hard."

"So you give up. Like you always do. You're pathetic."

Felix shifts uncomfortably.

Dad says nothing.

"Perhaps you and your father should have a conversation after I've left," he says. "But I really should explain to you what I want you to do. What the plan is."

"What the plan is?" Dad says. "Surely you want her to cut off all contact with this person?"

"Imagine she does, Mr Coady. What then? He'll just turn his attention to another woman, and we'll end up with another suicide we could have prevented."

"So what do you suggest?"

Felix turns his attention to me. "Harper, I know this is tough, but we need to catch this guy. I would like you to keep messaging him."

"What?" Dad says. "Are you crazy?"

"It's okay. We will add some software onto your phone and be tracking every word of the conversation. Our hope is that we can find out who he is, or try and track him via your messages."

"So you want to use her?"

"We will be doing the messaging. All we need from Harper is for her to make sure the messages sound like they are coming from her. If he suspects that we aren't Harper, if there is even some irregularity in her word choices, then we may lose him."

"Can't you just trace the IP address? Check the cellular tower the mobile phone uses or something?"

"It's not quite that easy. He's used a different IP address every time he's spoken to her, routed to various phones at different locations — he's done everything he can to prevent us seeing anything more than the messages he's sending to Harper."

I hate how they are talking about me like I'm not here. Like the decision's been made. Like I have nothing to do with this.

"Danny is a nice guy," I say, and even though I say it quietly, they seem to listen. "He's been nice to me when no one else has."

"I know he may seem like that, but he's just trying to make you think—"

"I won't do it."

Felix sighs. "You don't have a choice, Harper. If you don't agree, we already have a warrant to take your phone.

We'll have to do it without you, but I'd much rather do it with your help and cooperation."

So I don't have a choice.

They are going to use me to setup the only person who's ever made me feel special.

"Please go get your phone," Dad says.

"No."

"You heard the officer. They can to take it anyway whether you give it up or not."

"It's not fair."

"I know."

He smiles comfortingly and places a hand on my leg.

"Get your fucking hand off me!" I scream as I stand, marching to the stairs.

"Harper—"

"I will get you my phone! Then you can leave me the fuck alone!"

I march upstairs to my room and slam the door.

A few minutes later I come out with my phone and hand it over. The officer connects it to his laptop, does what he needs to do, and hands the phone back to me.

"You don't have to do anything," he says. "We will come back every day after school, and sit with you to go through the messages we'd like to send. In the meantime, if he messages you, act like you normally would, just don't give away any personal details. We'll be able to see all the messages you exchange. We just want you to be safe, Harper."

"Fine," I say, and go to my room, making sure they can hear the slam of my door.

I accept it, because they don't know.

They don't know that, in those few seconds it took for

me to get my phone, I was looking up Danny's phone number.

I was writing it down.

I will not betray Danny.

I will not hurt someone I love.

[28]
WILL

I often wonder how my life ended up like this.

I was a young adult with dreams of being a father and having a house full of love.

Now I have a child determinedly obsessed with an unknown stranger trying to groom her.

And what can I do about it?

Nothing.

"I'm sorry to put your family in this position," Felix says as he stands. He finishes his cup of tea and takes it into the kitchen, leaving it by the sink, and I follow him.

"It's okay. She's... going through a hard time. Me and her mother are splitting up."

"I'm sorry to hear that."

"Yeah. She already hates me enough right now, you know?"

Felix smiles. It's oddly comforting. Makes me feel like I'm not alone, which I know is stupid.

"You got kids?" I ask him.

"A daughter," he says.

"So I'm not the only one, then?"

He laughs. "If she spent as much time obsessing over her schoolwork as she did with boys, she'd be a genius. They just get to a certain age and have one thing on their mind, don't they? All she ever wants to do is go out with her friends and flirt."

I nod, if only to make it seem like I can relate.

I can't.

I've never known Harper to go out with boys. Not even once.

The first time I've known her to show interest in a boy is now, with a stranger on the internet, which isn't any more comforting.

I wish Harper could be a little more like Felix's daughter. Then I feel bad, knowing that I should love the daughter I'm given.

Which I do.

I just wish I could have done a better job, I guess.

I wonder how different things would be if I had.

"Well, I best be going," he says. "I imagine you have some books to mark."

That's odd. I hadn't told him I am a teacher.

Seeing the look on his face, he adds, "It's okay; I looked you up before I came. I'm a police officer, remember?"

Oddly reassured, I nod, and follow him to the door.

"I will be back tomorrow. Would four in the afternoon be too early?"

"No, that's fine, I can make sure I'm back by then."

"And hey — don't worry. Parenting isn't easy. You're doing a good job."

I force a smile. I appreciate his lie.

He opens the door. It's raining heavily.

"Thank you," he says, and shakes my hand. "Be seeing you."

He runs across the drive and gets into his car.

I close the door, shutting out the weather, and return to my warm, heated house.

I try calling Natalie. She should know what is going on, it's important. But the phone rings out to voicemail. I try again, and go to leave a message, then don't.

What would I even say?

If she cared, she'd call. She'd speak to her daughter.

I look up the stairs. Consider knocking on Harper's door. Talking to her. Comforting her in some way.

But what would I say?

I really don't know how to talk to her, which is awful. She's my daughter, yet I don't know her at all. I didn't even know that she was talking to a boy.

Am I a bad dad?

I scoff. Of course I am, don't be stupid. I'm useless. And Harper knows it, and that's what hurts the most.

I need to stop thinking.

It's best I leave Harper alone. Let her have her teenage angst. There's nothing I can do to help right now.

So I pour myself a glass of wine and sit in front of the television until I fall asleep.

[29]

HARPER

I wake up and behave just as I normally would.

I put on my school uniform, eat a bowl of Coco Pops, and ignore Dad's attempts to make idle conversation.

He offers me a lift and I turn it down.

There is nothing unusual about today.

Then, as Dad turns to go, he stops, and turns to me. He watches me for a few seconds, and I can imagine him rephrasing the same sentence in his head over and over until he comes up with the sentence that makes him sound the least pathetic.

"I'm sorry," he says. "For being such a rubbish father."

I wasn't expecting this.

"I shouldn't have gotten angry at you yesterday in front of the police officer. I know Mum leaving must be really hard on you. I know I should pay more attention, I just don't know how, and I..."

He trails off. Evidently this was not how he planned to say what he wanted to say.

"I'm trying, all right?"

Then, just as I'm starting to buy into his melancholy, he

says, "And I'm sorry you felt you had to speak to some boy on the internet because you couldn't speak to me."

Some boy?

Danny is not just *some boy*.

I wish everyone would see that.

"Goodbye, Dad," I say, and he finally leaves, and I head to school.

Then I walk straight past it.

And I get on the bus. Number 41 into town.

I take the coat out of my bag and put it on. It's a big coat; big enough to cover up my school uniform. I don't want anyone questioning why I'm not in school. The last thing I need is for the police to intercept me.

I put my headphones in and listen to something loud. The same shops and fields pass through the window as they always do on this route, and it occurs to me just how boring it must be to be a bus driver, always driving the same route. Then again, maybe they like the routine — there is comfort in the monotony of structure.

The bus at this time of the day is different than on the weekend. It's full of old women who take ages to hobble on, and either sit at the front, or recognise another old woman further back and talk to them. During the gap between two songs, I hear them talking, and I hear them listing names. I pause my music to listen, and it turns out they are going through all the people who have died since they last saw each other. I resume my music.

Twenty minutes later, the bus comes to a stop in town and I follow everyone off.

I keep my head down as I cross the high street. Everyone looks taller than me, and they either look at their phones or at their feet or at their lunch; nobody looks up. Ever.

I arrive at the EE store and someone is available to see me straight away. Ten minutes later, I walk out with a new pay-as-you-go phone. I'm going to have to figure out how to pay for it, but it's fine, it'll do for now.

I sit outside Costa amongst a load of men in suits, either on their phone or eating. The piece of paper with Danny's phone number is in my pocket. I take it out and enter it into this phone; it will be the only number it stores.

Danny, it's Harper.
I'm texting from another phone because the police are monitoring my other phone.
They say you're a bad person and they're after you.
What's going on?

I don't get a reply straight away, but he might be busy. If he's at school, he'll be in lessons, and the last thing he'll want is to have his phone confiscated, so I wait.

Ten, fifteen minutes pass, and soon it's an hour, and I've still heard nothing.

Have I scared him?

Does he believe it's me?

Should I not have said anything?

I find my way back to the bus and it drops me off at school in time for third period. I stare at my phone for the entire journey.

Beneath my message is the word *delivered,* but nothing else.

Third period is English. My teacher makes a comment about how I was marked absent this morning, and I tell them I was at the dentist. They say they'll make a note of it on the register, and that is how easy it is to get away with truanting — no wonder all those other girls do it.

After English, I make my way to Textiles, taking my phone out.

I have a text message and my heart beats faster, then I see it's not from Danny. It's from EE, thanking me for my business and letting me know what the costs of using my phone is.

I feel like crying.

I really hope I've not lost him. If I have, I'll never forgive Dad or that stupid policeman.

After Textiles is lunch, and still no reply. I sit at my table, alone as I always am, and eat whilst staring at the screen. I have it open on the message I sent, waiting for something to come up. Every time the screen begins to dim, I tap it to light it up again.

It reaches five minutes before the end of lunch and I pack my lunch box away. I feel like dying.

Then I see it.

Three dots that tell me he's replying.

The three dots remain for ages, and the bell goes, and people start to move, but I don't. I stay seated, waiting for the message.

And then it arrives.

FFS.

So sorry about that, Harper — you must be well freaked out.

I bought this phone second hand and didn't bother getting a new SIM card.

I keep getting all these dodgy messages from people.

*I'm pretty sure the last person who owned it was a
paedo or something.
Now they think I'm what?
Some kind of crazy guy?*

*I don't know.
They just said I have to write what they tell me.
So if you get messages from my old phone, it's the
police.
But this phone is just for us.
Only you have the number.*

You're amazing, you know that?

I'm not amazing.

*You are.
As soon as I saw your message I was worried I was
going to have to convince you, but you just know.*

That's because I know you, Danny.

*You do.
Like no one else.
And I promise I'll never hurt you.*

I know.

I would never hurt someone I love.

This message takes me by surprise.

A dinner lady tells me to get to my lesson, and I nod, and begin lifting my bag.

You love me?

With all my heart.

I love you too.

Then I am the happiest man alive.

And it doesn't matter what the policeman tells me to write later, or what the teacher does last period, or what Dad says — nothing will wipe this smile off my face.

I am in love.

Not the kind of love Mum and Dad had — this is *real* love.

And they would never understand.

[30]

WILL

She comes to see me again after school.

Again.

She's made me paranoid. Jumpy. I keep expecting another police officer to walk through my door, or for a parent to come charging into school, or for her to show up at my house.

She has no idea what she's doing to me. The torment she's causing. She has this infantile infatuation that she can't let go of, and has no idea it is making me scared of everything.

She kissed me, and whether I was consenting or not, I still will be perceived a certain way and I will lose everything.

Not just my freedom, but Harper.

Everything.

She closes the door behind her and I don't even bother to stop her anymore. She says, "Hi Will," and her voice is bouncy and she's wearing too much makeup and her ridiculous skirt is still too damn short.

I bow my head and bury it in my arms. If I can't see her, maybe she's not there; maybe she'll go away.

"Have you had a good day?"

I ignore her. Keep my head buried. Hope she gets the hint.

"Will, hello!" Her voice is still so happy, like she thinks I'm joking; like she has no idea she's deluded. "Come on, wakey wakey!"

She places a hand on my back.

"It's me!"

She places another hand on my arm and her arms wrap around me and I jump up, stepping out of her embrace and finally looking at her.

I catch sight of my reflection in the window. My shirt is untucked. My collar skewed. My hair a mess. I look like shit, and still she's obsessed.

She comes toward me again, tries putting her arms around my neck and leans in for a kiss and this time I don't just step away, I push her off, and my hand scrapes her breast as I do and the accident makes her giggle.

"Go away," I mumble, and she walks toward me again, but I move until there is a desk between us.

"But, Will..."

"Destiny, I don't want to talk to you."

"But I—"

"Dammit, what is wrong with you?"

"What's the matter? You seem flustered?"

It's genuine.

Her concern is actually genuine.

She's clueless.

Completely clueless.

No idea that I am not her boyfriend and she is not my

girlfriend and we are not in love and I am only a teacher who just wants to make it through the day.

She goes to walk around the desk to get to me, and I sidestep so the desk remains between us.

"What's the matter? Why are you avoiding me?"

"I don't know how many times I have to tell you this, but we are not a couple. I am your teacher, that's all."

She smiles again. That bloody smile.

"That's how it all started..."

"No!"

I'm shouting.

Someone might hear me.

Screw it, who cares?

I've had enough.

I'd had enough long ago, actually, and perhaps she's pushed me to the point at which I am shouting.

What have I done to deserve this?

I'm not even a good teacher. I don't spend time developing relationships with students, so why would one think I like them?

"I don't understand what's going on," she tells me.

"I am your teacher."

"And my—"

"Nothing! *Nothing!* I am your *teacher!* Your loser *fucking teacher!* Nothing else! *Nothing!*"

She is stumped. On the verge of tears. About to burst.

I don't care.

I really do not care.

I have started, and I am on a roll, and I will go on.

"I do not want anything to do with you besides marking your book and grading your bloody paper! We are not a couple; we are not in love — you are a student. *A student!* That is it, you hear me? *That is it!*"

She says nothing.

Her lip shakes. Tears dribble down her cheeks.

But she says nothing.

Then she reaches into her bag.

And pulls out a knife.

"What are you doing?"

I get ready to run, terrified she is about to use it on me.

But she doesn't.

She displays her wrist. Holds the knife over it and stares deep into my eyes; deep enough that she finds my soul, something that is buried far beneath my gut.

"Destiny, please…"

Her fingers flex over the knife. She tenses her muscles. Prepares herself.

"You're young, you're going to find a boy your age, I bet plenty of them are after you, I bet—"

She places the knife against her wrist and begins applying pressure.

"Stop it!"

A few speckles of blood ooze out of her skin.

"Fine, stop it, fine! Whatever! I'll be whatever, just stop!"

She lifts the pressure from her wrist and glares at me.

"Please, just, stop."

She waits a moment, and then says, "Tell me you love me."

I run my hands through my hair, huff, look around, try and find anything that will save me from this moment.

"Destiny, would you just—"

"Say it!"

She begins applying pressure again.

"Fine, fine!"

She pauses.

Watches me.

Waits.

And I'm going to have to say it. I have no choice; I am going to have to.

She raises her eyebrows expectantly.

"I love you," I mutter.

"I can't hear you."

"I said I love you. Now would you please—"

"Now tell me you'll always love me."

"Dammit, Destiny, would you—"

"Say it!"

I am sweating. It's dripping into my eyes, seeping through my shirt. I'm in a cold classroom, feeling like I'm standing among flames.

"Fine. I will always love you."

"And we'll always be together."

"And we'll always be together."

"And you will never lie to me again."

"Please, Destiny, I—"

"And you will never lie to me again!"

"Okay, fine, I will never lie to you again."

She holds the blade in place a few seconds longer, then she lifts it from her skin and holds it by her side.

She moves around the desk to get to me, and this time, I don't move out of her reach.

I just watch the knife.

She places her free hand on the side of my face and places a delicate kiss on my lips; one that, if it were from Natalie, I would saviour and cherish and feel it electrifying my entire body. As it is, this kiss makes me want to be sick, and I struggle to breathe.

She steps away and puts the knife back in her bag.

Her phone makes a noise.

She picks it up.

And, for a fleeting moment, I am sure that there is a message calling her by another name. Like Danny.

But her name is Destiny, and it looks similar, and I shouldn't be so ridiculous; she is crazy, not calculated, and I need to get a hold of myself.

She holds her phone to her face so I can't see it. Then she sees me looking worried.

"Don't worry," she says. "It's not another boy or anything. Just my dad. I have to go."

She types a message and puts her phone away.

"I will see you tomorrow, Will," she says, then places another kiss on my lips.

She turns and leaves.

There are a few drops of red on the carpet where she'd been standing.

I have to be home to meet Felix at four, but I can't leave the blood there, even just a few drops, it would pose too many questions, so I retrieve some bleach from the cleaner's cupboard and scrub it clean, then hurry home so I can be there for my daughter.

[31]

HARPER

You know that feeling when you're tuned into what's happening, but you aren't really paying attention? When you are aware enough to react to the words that are spoken to you, but in such a trance that you would not remember them?

That's what it's like. To sit here. With the police officer. Going through text messages he's prepared and confirming whether or not they sound like me.

Which is ridiculous.

Does anyone actually know what they sound like? Is anyone aware of the idiosyncrasies of their language, or what sociolect they use with different groups of people?

He asks me stupid questions, like, "Would you use a smiley here?" or "Would you abbreviate this word?"

I hadn't really thought about it, but Danny rarely abbreviates words. He never even says *rofl* or *lmao* or *lol*, he says *haha*. It's one of the reasons I love him; he never talks like a stupid person, even when texting.

I go along with it. I tell Felix how I think I would phrase a sentence and what words I wouldn't use.

Danny doesn't text back. He will when we're alone, when I can text him from the secret phone and let him know it's okay to talk.

Felix wants me to agree to meet Danny.

They want to use me as bait, like I'm a worm on the end of a fishhook and Danny's the trophy catch.

I say no.

Felix asks why.

Because I'm not ready yet.

In truth, I am both elated and terrified at the thought of meeting Danny. I would love to see him in person so I can know what it feels like to have his arms around me, but I would be petrified that he would see me and decide he'd made a mistake.

Either way, I am not going to meet him on the officer's terms. And I am not going to meet him so they can arrest the wrong person and put him in a cell.

I could tell Felix the truth. That Danny is innocent. That he has a second-hand phone and the last owner was dodgy. But I know what they'd say.

"Don't be so naive."

"That's what he wants you to think."

"Trust us, we've been onto this guy for a while."

And that's why I say nothing.

Neither Felix nor my dad know what it's like to be completely unheard. To be wanting to scream so loud they can't help but hear your voice, but knowing that, if you did, they would just cover their ears.

Dad doesn't even sit with us as we do this. Felix said that, due to my age, I have the right to have an appropriate adult with me. But I wasn't bothered about him being here, and he seems far too engrossed in something on the computer to even care.

Felix shows me some more messages. Asks me to check them.

He says he'll send them for me. I don't need to do anything but keep the phone nearby. They'll see everything that's done on the phone, so I needn't worry.

Except, it does make me worry. They have access to everything. All my messages. All my apps. They will know my high score on Candy Crush and they will see the photos I took of myself to send to Danny.

It makes me feel sick to think how keen they are to invade my privacy, and how much they thought I'd be happy to go along with it.

But I will go along with it.

For now.

Because I'm waiting to talk to you, Danny.

I'm waiting to let you know I'll never betray your trust.

Not now.

Not ever.

We are in love, and they will not understand.

[32]
WILL

I leave Harper and Felix to it. There's nothing I can do to help. I'd just get in the way.

And it gives me a moment, undisturbed, to search the internet for... Well, I don't know what. Information, I guess. A diagnosis.

I search for delusion disorders. The normal ones are there: psychosis, schizophrenia, delusional disorder.

They are all close, but not quite there.

I add keywords to my search; words like *relationship* and *convinced.*

And I come across a condition called erotomania.

The term sounds too close to 'erotic', as Destiny's behaviour is more obsessional than sexual, but the text beneath the headline strikes a familiarity:

A man or woman with erotomania is a person with a delusional belief that another person is in love with them, despite that person providing no indication or evidence that they are.

This is it.

I read on.

A person with erotomania will often focus on a celebrity, or a person of a higher status, such as a doctor or teacher.

They will believe that the object of their infatuation is confirming that they are in love too, such as through secret messages, and can be quite scary for the person they become obsessed with.

Scary?

Bloody right it's scary.

This is... her.

All of it.

It is just *her*.

Erotomania is uncommon, but when a patient with this paranoid delusion believes that the individual is in love with them, their behaviour can become obsessive and, often, dangerous.

The symptoms can start suddenly, but the fixation may not be immediately apparent. The object of affection, often an inaccessible older or higher status person who has previously had little contact with the patient, can remain unaware of the infatuation until the patient's behaviour becomes erratic.

I search for other websites associated with erotomania.

The first one that stands out is entitled *How to Spot the Symptoms of Erotomania.*

I click on it, although I'm fairly sure I could already guess the signs.

The stalker may make contact through written communication.

The stalker will believe that the object of affection is returning their love.

When the stalked makes it apparent that the attention is unwelcome, bizarrely, this can serve to confirm the stalker's love.

The stalker gets angry and threatening when told that their affections are not returned.

The stalker poses a threat to the stalked.

It's as if someone has watched Destiny and written down her behaviour.

I search for *erotomania cases.*

I regret it.

Immediately, there are such headlines as *Victim of Unwanted Affection Killed in Sleep*, and *Family of Stalked Murdered*, and *Erotomania Patient Murders Doctor for Denying Love*.

And that is when it becomes all the more alarming.

I'm thrilled that I've found an explanation — but now I am scared. Worried for what she might do, for how Harper might suffer because of it.

What if I showed this to Destiny?

What if I explained that this is what she has?

Maybe she would understand that it's not real. That she needs help. That it's a mental health issue, and not a sad tale of unrequited love.

I go onto Facebook. Out of curiosity, I type her name, *Destiny Hill,* and she is the first to come up in the results. Her profile picture shows her pouting at the camera. She's wearing a low-cut top you can see right down, and the skirt in her cover photo is as short as her school skirt.

"Dad?"

Harper makes me jump. I quickly close down the browser.

"I don't feel comfortable with this," she says.

"Uh huh."

"He's a good guy."

"Sure."

"Really, Danny isn't going to hurt me."

I don't reply. I don't have the energy for this argument.

"Officer Felix is going," she says.

"Okay, see him out for me."

"Don't you want to..."

She trails off.

Perhaps she sees me rubbing my eyes, or huffing, or

running my hands through my hair, and thinks I don't want to talk to her.

I do. I want to pay attention to her. I want to be a dad.

But when I turn around to tell her, she's gone.

Felix says his goodbye and goes.

I try calling out to Harper to come back, but she's already in her room.

I return my attention to the computer and print off all the pages I've looked at today. Once Destiny sees that there's a diagnosis for it, she'll realise it's wrong.

She will.

I'm sure of it.

She has to.

Doesn't she?

[33]

HARPER

That was it. That was my attempt at talking to Dad, at reasoning with him, at taking him at face value when he said he wanted to be more of a father.

He didn't take it.

And now I sit in my room, waiting for him to come up, to finish what he was doing and to come speak to me.

But he doesn't.

Why?

Why doesn't he?

It's not like he has loads of stuff going on in his life, and it's not like he's too busy, so there must be a reason he's too distracted to talk to me, there must be!

What is it?

I feel myself crying and I hate myself for it. I never want to give tears to someone who doesn't deserve it. I never want to let someone else have control over my emotions.

But what do you want me to say?

I'm alone in every way. At school. At home. And now they are trying to take away Danny.

Danny's right. Maybe Dad doesn't deserve to live.

Would it really be a loss to the world if he wasn't here?

I don't know if he's a popular teacher at his school, but I doubt it. I wouldn't like him as my teacher. If he's as neglectful of his students as he is of me then I doubt anyone would miss him if he was gone.

And I don't care.

I don't care if he doesn't care.

I don't care if he never talks to me or makes an effort. Once I reach eighteen, I am gone.

Only thing is...

I'm lying. I do care.

And I hate that I care. I despise myself for being unable to help it.

He's not overtly abusive, he's never laid a hand on me, or hurt me, or hated me, but he's never bothered to love me either.

I lie in bed. In the dark. Pull the duvet over me. And lie beneath it by the light of my secret phone.

I already have a message from Danny.

You okay?

Can't be easy having to deal with the police.

I'm sorry you're having to go through that.

Police are fine.

It's Dad.

What's he done now?

Nothing.

That's the point.

> *He's a waste of space.*
> *Stop wasting your time on him.*
> *Life would be far better if you stopped wanting him to*
> *be a part of it.*

I know.

You're right.

However much I agree, though, I can't help it.

I want a dad.

I find my teddy. The one Mum gave to me on the day I was born. She brought it to the hospital for me when she went into labour. It is small and brown and a little bit faded but I cuddle it nonetheless.

And I cry myself to sleep, holding the bear in my arms.

[34]

WILL

Fourth period arrives. The lesson I was both dreading and anticipating.

Destiny enters, giving me a subtle smile as she walks in and takes her seat at the back. I teach another mundane lesson going over previous exam papers with the occasional lecture about how their exams are imminent and they should show more interest. A boy stares out of the window and another chews his nails, and that's the most life I get out of them.

The bell goes and I dismiss them, but ask Destiny if she would stay behind.

"Of course," she says, in a way that probably seems inconspicuous to everyone else, but loaded with innuendo to me.

I check to see if anyone looks, or gives us another glance, if anyone's suspicious. No one cares. They are all just desperate to get to lunch.

She saunters up to me from her place at the back of the class, her blazer slung over her shoulder and held there by the tip of her forefinger. A button is open on her shirt and I can see the flowery pattern on her bra. I don't know if this is deliberate or not but I cannot show that I've noticed — she will interpret anything I do as confirmation of my love, and I need to ensure I do not say or do anything that can be misinterpreted.

"Sit down," I tell her.

"You want me to sit?"

"Yes."

I remain blank-faced. No expression in my voice. Nothing she can read into.

"Okay," she says, slightly confused, and perches on the edge of a seat at the desk closest to me.

She still doesn't cross her damn legs.

"Look at this," I say, and place the pages I printed off yesterday on the table in front of her.

She picks them up tentatively and reads.

"Erotomania?" she says.

"Yes."

"Is that to do with erotica? Because I—"

"Just read it."

She reads.

She lifts the first page away and puts it on the table, reading the next. And the next. And the next.

Until she gets to one page in particular and just stares, open-mouthed.

"What is this?" she asks.

"Well, I imagine it speaks for itself."

"Why are you showing me this?"

"Because it explains what's up with you, Destiny. You're sick. Ill. You need help. You are convinced that you are in love with me and that I am in love with you, but it's this... delusion. Called erotomania. It's—"

"What are you talking about?"

I pause.

"I'm talking about what you are reading."

"That has nothing to do with what I'm reading."

"Yes, it does. Unless you're not—"

She turns the piece of paper she's staring at around and shows it to me.

She's right, it's nothing to do with erotomania.

"Shit," I say. "No, that's not what I meant to show you."

"Are you checking up on me, is that it? You don't trust me?"

I bow my head.

I told my printer to print all the pages I'd been looking at.

I forgot that included her Facebook profile.

"No, Destiny, that is there by mistake—"

She stands. Holding it out. Looking confused. Completely disregarding the pages on the table about erotomania.

And I don't know what to say.

"This isn't going to work unless you trust me," she says.

I bow my head. Shake it.

"No, that's not what I meant."

"Unless, what, you wanted the pictures? Is that it?"

"No."

"Because you could have just asked."

"That's not—"

"You know, I wonder what your daughter would say if she knew she had more than one scumbag in her life."

"But, Destiny, I—"

Hang on.

Wait.

What?

"What did you just say?"

"I suppose it's actually quite flattering," she says, looking at her picture, her mood changing quite suddenly. "If you'd like, I could print this picture in colour, and frame it for you, and then you can keep it in your desk drawer. Not on your desk, I know, but you can take it out and kiss me whenever—"

"Destiny, stop. What did you just say?"

"What? About me framing this photo for you?"

"No. Before that. About my daughter."

"What about her?"

"What did you say?"

She shrugs. "I don't remember."

"Then remember."

"I don't—"

"Is it you?"

"Is what me?"

"Dammit Destiny, this isn't funny. Is it you?"

"I don't understand what you mean."

I can feel the rage firing through me. My arms are shaking, my knees are wobbling. I'm trying not to lose control.

"Are you Danny?"

"What? No, I'm Destiny."

"Are you the one texting my daughter?"

"I haven't texted—"

"*For fuck's sake!* Tell me the damn *truth!*"

I kick a chair over. I want to seem intimidating, but I know it just looks comical.

Either way, from the look on her face, she is taken aback. She is shocked by my aggression.

Good.

She should be.

"Tell me now. I mean it. Just tell me."

"Baby," she says, stepping toward me, putting a hand on the side of my face.

I hit it away. She grabs her arm, clutching the muscle I just struck.

I know I shouldn't hurt her, but it's tough, so tough, when I know what I just heard.

"This ends now."

"What do you mean?"

"I don't give a fuck about what you are doing with me — whatever you are doing with my daughter, you stop it."

"Will, you're scaring me."

"Good. I'm glad. You should be scared."

"But Will—"

"You hurt her, I'll kill you. You understand? I will kill you."

She looks stumped, at first. Shocked. Worried. Then her expression fades back into that stupid grin, that one she has that says *oh you're just being silly*, and she places her hand on the side of my face again.

"You're shaking," she says. "You're burning up. What's the matter?"

I am staring at her, wide-eyed and perplexed, not sure what else to say. What is going on?

What is the truth?

What is happening to my life?

"Enough," I say. "Go to lunch."

"I don't want to leave you like this."

"I'm fine."

"But—"

"I said *I'm fine!*"

A face hovers at the classroom door. A teacher. She asks if everything's okay. I go to tell her it's okay, but Destiny answers for me.

"I didn't do my homework, Miss. Sir's a bit angry."

The teacher nods and walks away.

"See?" she says, turning to me. "I'll always take care of you."

She leans her forehead against mine then kisses it.

Finally, she leaves.

I throw my coffee mug across the classroom, smashing it into pieces.

A few minutes later, I get the brush and dustpan and clear the pieces away.

[35]

HARPER

THE MORE I THINK ABOUT DAD, THE MORE I THINK
he'd be happier if he didn't exist.

Life is what he seems to hate most, and if it was taken
away from him, maybe things would be better; for both him
and me.

Danny texts me at lunchtime.

How's your day going cutie?

Okay. You?

Swell.
Lunch time detention for having my shirt untucked.
I'm sure my future employers will be devastated.

I laugh.

Then I get serious.

*You know the other day, when you were talking about
the best way to kill someone?*

Yeah.

Were you really joking?

Sure.
Why?

Sometimes I think...
I dunno.

It's your dad, isn't it?
He's a prick.
Ignore him.

You're right.

But you can't ignore him.
Can you?

No.

Then do it.
Kill him.
Make him suffer, or make it quick.

Are you joking again?

Do you want me to be joking?

I look at that last question for a while.

He doesn't text again. He waits for my reply.

But I don't know what to reply.

Just putting this into words, it's wrong... It feels all wrong.

Got to go.
Lunch is over.
Talk later.

Okay.
Love you.

Love you too.

The bell for next lesson won't go for another five minutes. I just want time to think.

I glance at the table adjacent to mine. Those girls with short skirts and dyed hair sit around boys with earrings and smooth skin.

My skin is blotchy and coated in acne, my belly rolls when I sit down, and I'm pretty sure my bra is too big. They make me feel stupid. Out of place. Like I don't belong.

And I guess I don't belong.

But I have a theory.

Those girls are like that because of their fathers. Their doting fathers, who heap money and presents upon them. Their fathers who they tell to go away when they give them attention, their fathers who tell them when their curfew is, their fathers who they slag off to their mates because they tried to help with their homework.

They have no idea how good they have it.

None of their fathers deserve to die.

I stare so gormlessly that the five minutes pass quickly and the bell goes. I sit at the back during Science, staring at the same girls who sit at the front and giggle and talk.

Even the teacher joins in with them, has a laugh with them, talks to them about nonsense that has nothing to do with osmosis. I know all about osmosis, I've answered all the questions from the textbook, I've done all the reading, but the teacher doesn't care. She wants to speak to the confident ones.

And, again, I wonder where their confidence comes from, but I know the answer: their fathers.

It's his fault I'm like this.

It's his fault I keep my head down and don't talk to anyone.

It's his fault that I have no friends, that teachers aren't interested in me, and that I go about my life unnoticed.

I walk home, lost in thought. I have tea with Dad, but he says nothing other than the obligatory "good day?" and "can you pass the ketchup?"

I lie in bed, staring at the last message between me and Danny and, before Felix comes over to draft more fake messages with me, I text the boy I love.

I've made up my mind.

About what?

I don't want you to be joking.

You don't?

You're right.
He's not a dad.
He's nothing.
The world would be better off without him.

His reply arrives just as the knock on the door comes from downstairs and I hear Dad greeting Felix.

I am so glad you said that.

[36]

WILL

There's another note on my desk the next morning. Not even in an envelope this time. She's getting reckless.

See you at lunch time?
Love you X X X X X X X

And below that is an imprint of her lipstick created by a kiss.

I teach her class first period. She sits at the back, her bag on her lap, and her phone behind it. Students often do this and think I don't notice. Of course I notice, I just don't care enough to tell them to stop. What's the point? Deny your education. Don't learn anything. What difference does it make to me?

Except now I am interested. She's texting someone. Who is she texting?

She keeps lifting her eyes from her phone and smiling at me. Like she knows I know. Like she's happy about it. Like she's smug.

I want to scream across the classroom, and I want to demand that she hands her phone over and tells me who she's texting. I have the right to do that as her teacher. I can confiscate a phone if she's on it. Demand to know who she's texting.

But what then?

I'm too afraid of her. If I say anything that upsets her then she goes blabbing away to the Headmaster and I'm in prison by dinner.

So she gets away with it.

When the class leave, she smiles at me, and says, "Goodbye sir," with that same silkiness to her voice. A few students turn their heads. They are beginning to notice.

Lunch time arrives, and I'm sat at my desk, brushing sweaty hair out of my face, staring at an email I've been trying to write for more than half an hour.

Destiny walks in and shuts the door. Puts her bag down. I take it and put it behind my desk so she can't get to any knife she might be holding.

This is the day it ends.

One way or another.

This is the day I break her until she won't want to love me anymore. If the only way to stop this is to hurt her, then maybe that's what I have to do. Not just for my sake, but for the sake of my daughter — if she is indeed pretending to be this Danny guy.

"How's your day?" she asks.

"Shit, Destiny. My day has been shit."

"Oh, why?"

She goes to massage my shoulders but I push her off.

She stumbles backwards and looks a little upset and it makes me a little pleased. Hopefully, the more upset she is, the more she'll hate me.

"Because of you."

"Me?"

"Yes. You are ruining my life, Destiny. Ruining it."

"But aren't I also the one who makes your day better?"

"No, Destiny, you're not. Your appearance yet again only makes it considerably worse."

"But—"

"Get this into your head, Destiny, we are not in love, we have never been in love, and we will never be in love. I am your teacher and I should have reported you a long time ago."

She looks at her bag. It's behind my feet. There is no knife for you to threaten me with now, you little bitch.

"You get like this sometimes," she says. "It's okay, I know what you're like. Sooner or later—"

"There is no sooner or later, you idiot. Don't you get it? I don't just not love you. I hate you. I despise you. I *loathe* you."

"You don't mean that."

She looks at her bag again.

I step forward, pushing her back.

"I rue the day you first walked into my class. I rue every day that you attended my lessons. I don't want to know you, Destiny, I don't want you in my life, I don't want you in my daughter's life. I want you to stop texting her, and I want you to leave me alone."

Tears accumulate in her eyes.

"But... You promised..."

"I promised nothing."

She looks at her bag.

"You're not getting to the knife," I tell her.

She reaches into a nearby tub of stationary. Takes out a pencil sharpener.

"What are you doing?"

She places the pencil sharpener on the table and hits it with her palm. It cracks. She takes the small blade from it and holds it over her wrist.

"Oh, for Christ's sake, Destiny, why?"

"Tell me you love me."

"Why, Destiny? Why? This is the question that I really can't get, that I've been racking my head about — why *me*?"

"It's always been you..."

"But why? I'm pathetic. I'm a useless husband, useless teacher, and as it's turning out I'm a pretty useless father too. I'm not whatever you think I am."

"You just don't see—"

"I'm nothing, Destiny." My voice quietens. My frustration turns to resolve. I feel my own eyes wavering as I hold back tears. "Nothing."

"Will..."

"I am not worth this. I am not worth your love, and I am certainly not worth your life. So put the blade in the bin and go. Please, just go."

She goes to cut herself but doesn't. Her arms drop to her side. The blade falls from her fingers.

She's crying hard. Mascara runs down her cheeks.

I lift her bag from behind me and hand it to her.

She takes it.

"Just go," I tell her. "No more of this. Please."

She doesn't say another word.

She turns and runs.

And I've never felt such relief in my life.

She's finally left. She's finally got it. She understands,

and she is done, and it's over, and I can finally return to the dull monotony of my meaningless life.

I feel unusually happy during last period. Even my students remark upon it. They are more attentive, and I remember what it was like to be the teacher I was when I first started. Back when I cared. Back when I wanted to change the world with education. When I had a wife with troubles we could handle together, and a baby with so much potential.

And the day ends.

And I'm ready to go home.

And that's when I get the email.

It's from the Headmaster, and he's asking to see me.

[37]

HARPER

FELIX SAID HE WON'T BE COMING BY TONIGHT. THAT HE
has enough to go on for today, and that he understands this
is difficult for me, and that he thinks I need a break.

It makes tonight the perfect opportunity, and that's
what I tell Danny as I walk home.

How should I do it?

Well, that depends.
Do you want it to hurt?

I just want to make sure I don't get hurt.

Then you might want to make it look like an accident.
Poison his food or something.

I don't really know where to get poison.

Anything can be poison.
Bleach.
Toilet cleaner.
Only problem is, he might taste something is funny
before he eats enough.
There is one way that is best.

What?

Stab him.
Get him in the throat then keep stabbing him.

Won't they know it's me?

Not if you phone the police afterwards and tell them you
found him that way.
Sound tearful.
Cry a lot.
Hand the knife to the officer who arrives so you can
explain why your DNA is on the weapon.

But won't it be suspicious if no one else's DNA is on it?

It can be explained.
And even if you are caught, you're under eighteen.
They'll lock you in young offenders for a bit then give
you a new identity when you're an adult.

Suppose.

Of course, you could always kill yourself afterwards.
Then no one will find you.

Kill myself?

But then I'll never get to meet you.

We'll still be in love.

That's what matters.

I mean…

This is crazy.

I can't believe we're actually talking about this.

Whatever you decide to do, I'll support you.

I believe in you Harper.

I pause at those words.

My thumb hovers over the screen, unable to reply.

He believes in me?

Suddenly, I am scared. Freaked out. Panicked.

What the hell am I doing?

Talking about killing someone…

I remember Mum telling Dad she believed in him. It was eight years ago. He was going for a job, and he was wearing a suit, and he was looking in the mirror and she was straightening his tie. I don't know why, but it's an image I've never forgotten. Perhaps because it's the only time I've ever seen Dad happy. Mum got pretty sick after that.

But Dad never relented. He took care of her, and he kept taking care of her over and over. He never stopped.

Maybe that's why he struggles to take care of me. Because he's worn down by how much he's had to take care of her.

Maybe I'm not being very understanding.

I don't think I can do this.

That's fine.
Not forcing you.
I just want to help.

I know you do.

I go to type something else, only to find that I don't know what I'm typing.

This talk of murder is getting really heavy.

I love Danny, but I need a break from this talk. Not from him, but from this conversation.

I'll talk to you later tonight.

Okay.
Love you.

Love you too.
So much.

I turn my phone off and put it in my bag.

I walk past a group of girls who are laughing, loudly, and although they aren't looking at me, I'm sure it's at me, even though it's probably not, I just don't know; it feels like everyone's always laughing at me and I can never tell whether someone is actually mocking me or not.

I drop my head. Cover my ears to keep the noise out and rush home.

[38]

WILL

I arrive at the Headmaster's office and, just as I go to knock, I hear that shrill voice again.

"Can I help you?"

The Headmaster's secretary has a phone in her hand. She struggles to grip it because her fake nails are almost as big as her fake eyelashes.

"He's asked to speak to me."

"I'll let him know you're here, please take a seat."

"But he's asked—"

"He's with a student right now, please take a seat and I'll let him know you're here."

I glare at this woman for a moment, wondering what she would do if I just walked straight in. I have a degree, a master's degree, and a post-graduate certificate in education, yet this vain, inept woman who can only recite the same sentence over and over thinks she can dictate what I do.

But, being the sad sack that I am, I meander over to the seat and I sit down.

My arms fold. My foot rests on my knee. My eyes travel to the clock.

She picks up the phone and tells the Headmaster that I'm here so loudly that most people in the building probably heard it. She's the kind of person who doesn't have a quiet voice; yet another reason I despise her.

Ten, fifteen minutes go by and I feel more and more agitated. I try to stop my leg from shaking, but it doesn't stay still for long.

Eventually, the door opens.

It stays open for a moment, then someone walks out of it.

Destiny.

She glances at me then keeps her head down, scuttling out; all part of the performance where she plays a timid, innocent girl, and hides the psychotic beast that hides within.

The Headmaster steps out of the door. He looks at me. Grim expression. Pretending to hate what he's about to do.

"Come in, please, Will," he says, and I do so.

He shuts the door behind us. I notice a picture of him and his daughter on the desk. He notices me looking at it and shoots me a look, like I'm a predator, like I should not be looking at a picture of a young girl.

"Sit down," he tells me.

I sit on the seat opposite his desk and I sink low. This seat feels smaller than it did a few days ago.

"I'm going to give you an opportunity to talk," he says. "For you to tell me what is going on before I relay what has been disclosed to me."

I say nothing.

"Will, I really don't want to do this, so please, just make this easy for me."

"I have done nothing wrong," I tell him. "Everything she's just told you is a lie."

"Okay, well let me go through a few things. She said that you printed off her Facebook profile."

I go to reply, but can't.

"She says you have shouted at her whilst being shut in a classroom alone with her."

Again, only stutters come out.

"She says that you kissed."

"No, that's not — she kissed me. She tried to."

"She tried to?"

"Yes. I stopped her."

"Then why haven't you reported it?"

I don't have an answer.

He bows his head in his hands.

"Will... This looks really bad..."

He's hating this, but not as much as I am.

"She says you're in a relationship," he tells me.

"She's convinced we are, but I promise you, we are not. She has erotomania."

"What? Eroto — what is that? Some sort of erotic act?"

"No, it's not. It's an obsessive delusion."

"Cut it out, Will."

"I'm not lying."

"Yes, but I doubt you're telling the truth either. Can you really give me an explanation to what she's told me?"

I can't.

Whatever I say, it will be misconstrued.

And I know I can't say anymore.

"I need to speak to my union," I say, and he laughs; not a laugh of genuine hilarity, but of awkward surprise.

"Okay, Will, let me tell you what is going to happen. You are going to be suspended from teaching, immediately, and will not be permitted to enter school grounds, pending investigation. We will be passing what we have onto the police, who will no doubt want to speak to you. I just..."

He shakes his head. Leans toward me.

"What were you thinking? She's a child, Will."

What am I supposed to say?

I stand up. Walk to the door without looking back.

Within ten minutes I've packed my things and I'm gone, staring at the school in the rear-view mirror, wondering if I'll ever return.

[39]

HARPER

I hear Dad arrive but I don't leave my room.

I don't ever want to leave my room.

Only, I hear Dad talking, with vehemence and passion I've never heard, almost with aggression, and my curiosity becomes too much.

I open my door, only slightly, and listen to what he is saying.

"No, a lawyer... It's a lawyer I need... Your website says you specialise in this kind of thing... Well don't you?"

A lawyer? Why would Dad be talking to a lawyer?

I step out of my bedroom and walk down the stairs, stepping lightly, not only to mask my presence but to ensure I can hear every bit of the conversation.

"No, yes, I mean I did kiss her, but I didn't, she kissed me... She forced it on me, I didn't — that's why... No, it wasn't like that..."

She kissed me?

Who did Dad kiss?

Did he cheat on Mum? Was that why she left?

I reach the bottom step, but I don't move any closer to

the living room. He appears by the doorway then disappears again, pacing back and forth, too involved in his conversation to notice me.

"She's sixteen, at the age of consent, yes, but I was her teacher — *am* her teacher, or would be, I don't know... No, of course not! ... She's a psycho. She has erotomania, she was obsessed with me..."

Sixteen?

He's her teacher?

He kissed one of his students?

That student could be one of the girls laughing at me, or joking with the teachers, or she could be like me, walking home alone and hating their parents.

And Dad is just another predator in her life.

"Yes, I found her Facebook profile, but it was a mistake... I printed it off, yes, but I swear I wasn't stalking her..."

Her Facebook?

He's lying. He was stalking her.

Why else would you go on her Facebook? And print it off?

I mean...

I thought Dad was a piece of shit. But I never thought he was a stalker. An abuser. A paedophile.

I never thought he was a man who would have harmed one of his students.

"Quite a few times I've been alone with her... Yes, I know it's my word against hers, but what happened to presumed innocent before found guilty? ... To hell with the jury, that's not fair... Look, will you represent me or not? ... No I have not been arrested yet, but they are passing it on, so it's just a matter of... Fine, okay, call me back... That's fine. I'll be in all evening... Well, hopefully... Goodbye, thank you."

He hangs up. Just stands there. By the fireplace. A hand on his hip and the other on his head. Staying very still, until he throws the phone across the room with a scream.

That's when he sees me. Standing at the bottom of the stairs, looking at him in a way I've never looked at him before, staring at the man I thought couldn't get any lower in my estimation, but found a way to access the lower depths of humanity.

My dad. Abuser. Groomer. Stalker.

God, even rapist for all I know.

Am I even safe with him here?

Is anyone?

He says nothing. Doesn't offer an explanation. Just stares at me.

Then his mouth does open, but I don't want to hear it, so before he can say anything, I run upstairs and shut myself in my room.

I was wrong to think he didn't deserve to die.

In fact, I've never met anyone more deserving.

I pick up my phone and text Danny. He can tell me what to do next.

[40]

WILL

HARPER LOOKS AT ME, AT FIRST, WITH A CURIOUS peculiarity. A vague sense of intrigue, or a senseless interest.

But then it changes.

And I wonder how much she heard as her expression morphs into that of disappointment, and the way she sees me becomes so apparent.

I know she doesn't look up to me. I know she doesn't admire me, or see me as a role model, or someone from whom she craves affection. But I at least hoped she thought I wasn't a complete bastard.

But she does now.

Oh, how she does now.

I go to explain, but she runs upstairs and doesn't give me the chance.

I should go after her.

I should.

But I don't.

I stand in the darkness of the living room. It's not that late, but there's a storm raging outside, and it leaves little light. I don't turn the light on, not wanting the headache that the light will bring, instead preferring to remain in the grey and the shadows that the storm has granted me.

The cabinet is where we keep the nicer drinks. Not the cheap wine Natalie left, but the whiskey and the brandy and the port and the sherry, and I take a tumbler and fill it to the brim with the first bottle I find.

The colour is a brown transparency. A gulp and the sharp sting against my throat tells me it's whiskey. I don't care so long as it numbs every feeling I have.

Lightning strikes. Thunder roars. All the cliches about the torrential elements come true, and I hear nothing but the rain battering the house.

I refill my glass and wander to the window.

I'm almost waiting for the police car to arrive. For an officer to come and arrest me. To confiscate my belongings, ready to search my phone and computer for incriminating evidence that proves I'm the predator I'm being made out to be.

I wonder if Felix will make the arrest, or whether someone else will do it.

I wonder what the charges will be.

Sexual assault? Grooming? Predatory behaviour?

Is predatory behaviour even an offence?

The flower bed I planted with Natalie gets destroyed by the violent downpour. The petals fall off and the stems wilt as bullets of rain destroy them.

I take another sip.

It's sharp. It stings, but not as much as the first sip.

A car drives by the end of the drive. I wonder who's in it. Some father, perhaps taking his daughter home. I stare at the space it temporarily occupied, waiting for another car to drive past.

Then I see it, beyond the elements, amongst the weather's punishment; a figure. A silhouette, stepping tentatively forward, emerging.

It's a girl's outline.

It stops at the end of the drive. Looks in this direction, though I can't see the face.

I peer harder, but I already know who it is.

She's found my house.

Now she's not only invading my work, she's invading my home. No part of my life is safe.

I think of Harper upstairs, and I can't let Destiny in, I can't let her get any closer; I can't let her get to my daughter.

Harper is all that matters.

I place my drink on the windowsill and make my way to the front door.

I open it.

I stare at the figure, waiting for it to move, but it doesn't. She hovers, not coming any closer, but not going any further away.

"What are you doing?" I shout, but the storm is too loud and my voice is lost.

I shout louder.

"Why don't you fuck off and leave us alone?"

Stupid move.

She can't hear me, but Harper can.

I step onto the drive, leaving the door open behind me.

I don't take a jacket. It takes a few seconds until I'm drenched, soaked, my clothes clinging to my skin, my hair dripping water into my eyes.

"Please," I say.

She doesn't move.

I edge closer.

She's wearing a dress.

Nothing but a dress. A short, summery one, that clings

to every bit of her body. I can see the outline of her hips, her waist, her breasts.

Her bare legs are smooth and wet.

She's doing this deliberately. She's wearing a dress that she knew would be revealing. She wants to tempt me.

She's psychotic.

"Destiny, what are you doing?"

She still doesn't reply.

I walk toward her.

[41]
HARPER

I hear Dad shouting.

I also hear the storm outside and the silence in my room.

I stand in front of the mirror. Staring at myself with my bushy hair and frumpy skirt and blotchy skin and the thought that Dad created me makes me hate him even more.

I pick up my phone.

Danny?

I'm here.

What do I do?

What do you mean?

How do I do it?
I don't know how.
I'm scared.

You mean your dad?

He's a paedophile, Danny.
He's abused a girl at school.
I heard him talking on the phone.
I can't believe it.

What did I say?
He deserves to die.

You're right.
I have to stop him from hurting anyone else.
I have to do what's right.

I'll be with you the whole time.

What do I do?

Have you got sharp knives in the kitchen?

Yes.

Get one.
Do it now.

With my phone trembling in my hand, I leave the comfort of my room and begin the long journey down the stairs, the tufts of an ageing carpet sticking between my toes.

I reach the bottom step. The front door is open. The rain is belting down and it's wide open. Why has he left it open?

Then I realise — he's outside. Walking slowly across the drive.

I walk through the living room, past the open drinks cabinet, and into the kitchen.

The knife block is next to the oven. Below the cupboard where the fancy plates are. The ones we use when we have guests.

The ones we haven't used in years.

There are four knives. Various sizes. Various degrees of sharpness.

I find the biggest one and take it out.

I turn it over, twisting it, staring at it. I'm transfixed by its lack of beauty. It cuts vegetables and it kills fathers. Its only purpose is to slice things apart.

You there?

My phone vibrates.

Danny's with me.

Through all of this, he's with me.

And I know he won't leave my side.

Yes.

You have it?

It's in my hand.

Look at it.

Admire it.
Feel it like it's part of your body.
Your weapon should be an extension of your arm.

I don't know what he's talking about, but I try.

I don't know how to admire a knife. I don't know how to make it part of my body.

I place the side of the cool blade against my neck.

It's hard. Rigid. Definite.

It's sharp.

Now go to him.

I return to the front door.

Dad's lost in the rain, but I can make out the outline of his body, somewhere amongst the downpour.

What if I can't do it?

You have to.

But what if I can't?

Be strong, Harper.

But what if it's too difficult?
What if I'm not strong enough?

There's another thing you can do.
Something that will cause your dad more pain than
death.

What?

You can kill yourself.

This stumps me.
Why would he want me to do that?
How would we meet?
How would we be in love?

I don't understand.

The only other way to hurt him is to take yourself away
from him.
He'll live with regret for the rest of his life.
It'll be a fate worse than death.
It's him or you, Harper.
I believe in you.
And I love you.

If you love me, why would you want to lose me?

I want what's best for you.

But I don't want to die.

But you don't want to live.

I look from my phone, to the knife, to Dad, to the phone to the knife to Dad, to the phone to the knife to the phone to the knife to the phone to the knife and I drop it.

The phone. The knife.

I drop it.

It's clatter on the floor is louder than the storm.

I stare at my father in the rain.

And I step out of the house, walking toward him.

[42]
WILL

"What are you doing here, Destiny?" I shout. The rain is coming down even harder, if that's possible. It's difficult to hear my own voice.

I'm sure she's crying, but I can't tell. The rain has dragged her makeup across her face and you can't even tell if she's pretty or not anymore.

"I told them I lied," she eventually replies.

"You what?"

"After the Headmaster saw you, I went back. I told him I lied."

"Why would you do that, Destiny?"

She shrugs. Looks around for the answer.

There's something new in her voice. Whininess mixed with resolve. Sadness, but not at the notion of losing me, but perhaps at what she's done.

"I just wanted you to know how it feels," she tells me.

"How what feels?"

"For someone to not believe you. To call you deluded. To call you a liar."

"So it's payback, is that it?"

"But now you know how it feels, we can finally be—"

"But you *are* deluded, Destiny."

"No!"

I step toward her.

"What you told the Headmaster was lies. What I told you was the truth."

"Truth is only what you believe it to be."

She tries to cup my face and I whack her arms away. It hurts her, but I don't care.

"I do not love you. You are a child. A psychotic. A deranged lunatic who belongs in an asylum, not a school."

"Why are you saying these things?"

I step forward again, until my body towers over hers. She is pressed against me, but there is nothing romantic about it, and I can see from the look on her face that she is scared.

Good. She should be intimidated.

"I cannot stand you. You wear skirts too short and pretend not to realise. You unbutton your shirt to show off your bra. You walk around like everyone should desire you, but they don't, Destiny."

"Will, please..."

"Boys will use you. They will. But not because they love you — because they can."

"Will, stop!"

She goes to turn away, but this time it's me who isn't letting her go; this time it's me who grabs her arm and pulls her back.

"Let me tell you what's going to happen. You are going to stop bothering me, and you are going to stop texting my daughter. You come near her again, you so much as send her another message — I will kill you. Do you understand? I will—"

"Dad?"

A faint voice from behind me.

I turn around and there she is. Harper. Drenched just like me. Standing a few steps behind, looking so vulnerable.

I want to put my arms around her and protect her from everything. Instead, I expose her to the true evil of the world.

I step back, hold my arm out to indicate Destiny, and say to her, "This is him, Harper."

"What?" she says.

"This is the boy who's been texting you," I tell her. "This is Danny."

[43]

HARPER

I STARE AT THIS GIRL, A LITTLE OLDER THAN ME, BUT
looking just as scared.

"What?"

"This girl," Dad says, "has been masquerading as
Danny. She has told lies about me, that I have been inappropriate with her, but none of it is true."

"She can't be Danny, though. She can't be..."

"She is. Why don't you ask her?"

I look at this girl. Shivering. Holding her arms around
herself. Wearing a dress that clings to the perfect curves of
her body.

"Is this true?" I ask her.

She doesn't reply.

"Answer me!" I'm shouting. I've never heard myself
shout like this, and it hurts my voice, but I don't care.

The girl doesn't reply.

"Tell me!" I demand.

The girl looks down.

I turn to Dad. He looks so smug. So pleased with

himself. I expect to see sympathy for my predicament, but I only see pleasure that he's exposed the truth.

"And you knew?" I say.

"Yes," he says, his voice small.

"And you didn't tell me?"

"Would you have listened if I did?"

I turn back to the girl. I've had enough of Dad. I know he's a lousy parent, but I didn't think Danny would be...

This.

"How could you?" I ask.

She shakes her head.

"Answer me!"

"Please," Destiny says. "Just... This wasn't meant to hurt you..."

"And you told me to... do that to him? That was you?"

She shakes her head.

"Don't lie!"

She looks down.

I look back at Dad.

And I rush inside, pick up my phone and run upstairs, shut my door, shut out the world, shut out everything.

I don't want to see them. I don't want to see anyone ever again. I'm so sick of this world, this life, the constant pain of living. No one I rely on is truly ever there.

My phone lights up. I have a text message. It's from Danny.

I tell myself not to read it. What good could come?

But I can't help it.

Fine.

You won't do it?

I will.

I'll kill both of you.

You had your chance, Harper.

Remember that.

YOU HAD YOUR CHANCE.

The phone drops from my hands.

I rush to the window. They are both still there.

I run back downstairs.

[44]
WILL

"It's over," I tell her. "I'm going inside."

"Wait!" she says, and she takes something from inside the back of her dress. It's an envelope. She hands it to me.

"I don't want it."

"Take it."

"No."

"Take it and I'll never bother you again!"

Reluctantly, I take it. "Now get off my property."

I turn and walk toward the house. My back toward her. Refusing to look behind me. Refusing to dignify her with another moment of my time.

I feel something rush toward me, toward my back, and I glance over my shoulder — but it's just the wind.

I return inside the house, shut the door, and almost slip on something. A knife. On the floor. I pick it up and wonder why it's there.

My eyes turn to the stairs where Harper is staring at me, not quite at the bottom but not at the top either. It's funny, isn't it, how we always know when someone is looking at us?

Even though we don't speak, I feel like we understand each other in this moment better than we ever have before.

"Who was she?" Harper asks.

I look at the knife I'm holding in one hand, and the envelope in the other. I want to explain everything, but I feel strange that I'm holding these things, like it makes this conversation more sinister than it should be.

"One minute," I say, and I take the knife to the kitchen, where I place it in wooden block, then put the envelope on the side. I pause, wondering what I'm going to say to my daughter.

When I turn around, she's waiting behind me.

"Her name is Destiny," I tell her.

"Is she the one you had an affair with? Is that why she did that?"

"I didn't have an affair, Harper."

"But I heard you on the phone—"

"Then you heard wrong."

I regret snapping as soon as I say it.

"She was obsessed with me. She has something called erotomania — it's when you're convinced that someone is in a relationship with you when they aren't. She really believed I loved her, and she tried to kiss me, Harper, that is all. I told her no."

"Did you report it?"

"I... didn't."

"Why not?"

"I was scared."

She scoffs.

"It's not as simple as it sounds," I insist.

"Sure."

"It isn't. For starters, she threatened to hurt herself with a knife. Secondly, do you know what an accusation can do?"

"But if you're innocent..."

"I am innocent, and she accused me, and already you don't believe me. How would I convince you if it went one step further and the police arrested me?"

Harper nods. Faintly. A small movement of understanding that means so much to me.

"So why did she pick on me?"

I shrug. "I don't know, Harper. Honestly. Perhaps to mess with me, or to get her own back for me rejecting her, or as part of her sick game. Maybe she actually thought she was this Danny boy."

She looks down at the phone in her hand. It's silver. I thought her phone is black.

Oh god... It isn't her phone...

"What is that?" I demand.

"Don't get mad."

"Mad about what?"

"I said don't get mad."

"Mad about *what*?"

"If you get cross with me, I'll go up to my room and this conversation will end. I'm only talking to you if you're going to be understanding."

Understanding?

The idea seems preposterous.

But still, she's right. This is the most we've spoken in months, possibly even years. I like it, even if it's under the wrong circumstance. If I want to keep it going, I need to be patient.

"Fine," I say. "Tell me."

"It's another phone I got, and I only gave Danny the number. It was so I could still speak to him... You know, in private..."

"Even after Officer Felix told you—"

"Danny didn't seem like a bad person. I didn't believe Felix."

I fold my arms and lean against the table.

"What changed?"

She looks down at the phone, and back to me again. She looks like a child in trouble. Like she did when she was six and she'd done something naughty but was too afraid to tell us.

"He sent me a message."

"A message?"

"Yes. I need to show it to you."

She unlocks her phone and presents the screen to me.

[45]

HARPER

I DON'T LET DAD SEE ANY OF THE OTHER MESSAGES. None of the ones about killing him; I'm not ready to go there yet. I just show him the last one.

The one where Danny says he's going to kill Dad.

The one where Danny says he's going to kill me.

Dad doesn't say anything, at first. Initially, he seems angry, then he seems despondent, then he seems... I don't know. I don't know his expressions anymore.

I did once, but not now.

"Why don't you begin from the start," he says. "Why don't you tell me everything?"

So I do.

Aside from the part about killing him, I tell him every detail of our conversations, about what he — or she — said to me, how they loved me, how I'm special.

How he gave me what Dad never did.

When I say that, I stop, and let it linger. There is a sadness in his face, and it makes me happy, in a way; that he cares enough to be hurt by it.

"I'm sorry," he says, and he wipes his eyes even though

there's no tears, but I can see them glistening, I can see him trying. "I'm sorry you felt you couldn't talk to me. I'm really sorry, Harper. I am. I'll be better. I mean it. I know I've said it before, but I'll be better. I'll be the dad you need. I promise."

I hug him. He smells like rain. His hair drips onto my top, but I don't care.

I didn't realise just how much I wanted this.

It doesn't last long, though, as he pulls away and wipes his face.

"What should we do now?" I ask.

"I'll phone Officer Felix. See if he can bring some police presence, or someone to watch us, or... I don't know. Let us know what to do."

"Okay."

"Then I think we should both stay downstairs. Together. Yeah?"

I nod. He hugs me again.

Then, just as he's about to step out of the room to find his phone, something occurs to me.

"Dad?"

"Yeah?"

"How did Destiny send those messages?"

"I don't know, from her own phone I guess."

"No, I mean, her last message, the one where she says she's going to kill us... How did she send it?"

"What do you mean?"

"She was outside with you at the time. Did you see her on her phone?"

He's suddenly lost in thought. He looks at me, but he's not there; he's going through all the possible explanations and rejecting each one.

"I don't know," he finally concludes. "Curious."

"Isn't it strange?"

"Yes. But she could have found a way. She could have timed the messages to send or something, I don't know."

"I'm not sure if you can do that."

"I think the best thing is to get Officer Felix here, then he can help us figure it out. Don't worry about it for the moment, okay?"

"Okay."

With a forced smile, he leaves. Seconds later I hear him talking on the phone, but I tune it out, lost in thought.

I open my phone again and read the messages.

I'll kill both of you.
You had your chance, Harper.
Remember that.
YOU HAD YOUR CHANCE.

I had my chance?

Was this his intention all along? To get me to join The Death Club like Linda Salborough?

I've got to stop referring to Danny as him. It wasn't him. It was *her*. And, by the sounds of it, she was a sick person.

Dad re-enters the room and I quickly put the phone away.

"He's on his way," he says. "Shouldn't be too long. Says we should stay together while we wait. Sounds like a good idea, don't you think?"

I nod. I don't want to be alone.

"We could watch a movie. You still into Disney?"

"I'm fourteen, Dad."

"That's a shame, I just bought Disney Plus. Figured we could find something on there."

I smile. He's trying. "That would be good."

"Well, hey, why don't you make us both a cup of tea? I just have to go do something in the other room, then I'll be right back."

"I thought you said we should stay together."

"And we will, I'll just be two minutes, I promise."

He smiles another forced smile, grabs an envelope from the kitchen side, and rushes into another room.

Strange, really, how he can make me feel so loved then so alone within seconds.

I put the kettle on and begin making the tea, gazing out of the window as I do, trying to decipher the various shapes of the storm.

[46]
WILL

I TAKE A SEAT BY THE COMPUTER, PLACING THE SOGGY envelope down. From here, I can hear Harper in the kitchen, the occasional closing of the cupboard door and placement of a mug on the side.

I open the envelope Destiny gave me and take out an A4 scrap book. The cover is leather bound but dog eared, and the pages inside are a dark cream colour. But it is not the condition of the book that bothers me. It is the photograph of me on the first page. It is a copy of my staff photograph from work.

On the next page are more photos. Me getting out my car in the morning. Me carrying a box of books through the corridor. Me through the window of my classroom, teaching.

These aren't just recent photos — they go back to the beginning of the year. Months ago.

Destiny may have only begun inappropriate contact with me in the past few weeks, but this obsession seems to have been going on for months. At least.

On the next page are pieces of paper torn from her exercise books. They have comments by me such as *Good work, Destiny* and *Keep it up* and *This is really good stuff, keep working hard.*

Every compliment I've ever written in her book for good work is stuck to these pages.

On the next page. Natalie. In a pub. In a club. Without me, but never alone. In each picture, a large X in red marker covers her face.

On the next page... Harper.

Sitting alone at a table surrounded by full tables. Is this at lunch time? Is this how it is for her? She eats alone?

God, I've neglected my child. I don't even know enough to see she's beyond lonely. She's an outcast. She's friendless, and she's not even being bullied — worse, people are indifferent to her. She's unnoticed.

On the next page is list of lessons, and what I was wearing on that day, what kind of things I said, and whether I chose her when she put her hand up to answer a question.

Finally, the following page is divided into two. To the right are pictures of me. To the left are pictures of her.

Each picture of her seems to have been cut out from another picture. There are the edges of other people in the picture, but they've been removed to make way for me.

One picture draws my attention. A large arm is around her, but the owner of that arm has been cut out. The arm is big. Muscular. Far older than one of her classmates.

It's weird, but that arm's familiar.

"Dad, tea's ready!"

"I'll be there in a minute — why don't you get the TV on!"

I log onto the computer. Open the internet browser. Find Facebook.

Despite how much I regretted doing this before, I search for Destiny Hill again.

Something compels me to find this photo. To find who she was with. To see who the arm belongs to.

Her profile loads up. I click on photos.

They are full of selfies with pouting lips and excessive cleavage and shots in the mirror of her wearing tiny skirts. Some pictures have friends in, but the focus is always on her. She is the dominant feature of the photograph, the one who draws your eye; everyone else is just there to make her look better.

There is a knock on the door.

Harper walks past and I quickly turn off the monitor.

The door opens and closes, and Harper calls out, "Officer Felix is here!"

That was quick.

I turn off the monitor, place the envelope under the computer desk, and go to greet him.

[47]

HARPER

I explain everything to Felix, and Dad sits with me. He's distracted, but it's fine. Sitting next to me is more support than he's ever done before. My English teacher always says any progress is good progress.

Once I've finished, Felix sits back in the armchair, his hand resting on his chin, looking thoughtful. His cup of tea remains untouched, but he picks up the hobnob and bites half of it.

Once he's finished eating, he speaks.

"Okay. Right. Thank you for telling me this, Harper, it... it, well..."

He wants to tell me I was foolish for getting another phone. I can see it. The words have met his lips, he's just not saying them.

"I'm pleased you've told me the truth now, at least. And you say this Destiny girl is behind it?"

"Yes," Dad interjects. "She came here and I confronted her."

"And she admitted she did it?"

Dad glances at me. She never actually said those exact words, but we took it as an admission.

"As good as," he says. "I know it's her."

"Right, well, the best thing is if you show me the messages, and we can go from there. Myself or another officer will stay here for the time being, until we have enough to question her."

"When will that be?"

"Hopefully once you've shown me the messages. Then I can make the call. Shall we?"

I look at Dad, and he nods. A little assurance that it's okay. The police officer is here now. He'll protect us.

"Why don't we sit at the table in the kitchen and do it?" Felix suggests. "Would be easier."

We get up and head toward the kitchen, but Dad lingers.

"I'll be with you in five minutes," he says. "I just need to finish something on the computer."

It annoys me at first that he is not going to be there, supporting me, then I think it's probably best — I can tell the officer about how they tried to make me kill Dad without him knowing.

God, even just to think those words... *Make me kill Dad...* What was I thinking?

Dad leaves us to it and we take a seat at the table. Felix takes out a laptop, connects a wire, and holds his open palm out to me.

After I look a little confused, he prompts me by saying, "The phone, Harper."

I stare at this hand.

Something about the way he says it unnerves me. It's the demanding nature of it. It's not a request, it's not supportive, it's... forceful.

Shouldn't he be taking the phone to the police station? Shouldn't he be calling someone? Shouldn't he be getting an expert to do this?

Still, it's not up to me to question how the police do things. I don't know what the protocol is.

So I hand the phone over.

He plugs it into the computer and loads the text messages.

[48]

WILL

I peer through the hallway before I turn the monitor back on and listen. They are talking in the kitchen. I can't hear what they are saying, but I know they are there.

I wonder if Felix knows about Destiny's accusations. Did she tell the Headmaster she was lying before he contacted the police? Would he contact the police anyway? And would they make Felix aware?

He isn't acting any differently toward me. In fact, he's quite eager to help. If he knows something, he isn't giving it away.

Destiny's Facebook profile appears once again on the screen. Photo after photo of vanity and self-indulgence.

There are more than a thousand photos. It's going to take me more than five minutes to go through them all.

Surely it must be a recent one. Surely I won't have to go too far back...

I keep scrolling. Past photos of her in the park with her friends a few weeks ago. I wonder if she was thinking about me at that time, planning on approaching me, or if she was already convinced we were in love.

Past photos of her outside a house. I remember her parents have recently divorced, and she stands with an older woman who I assume is her mother; this must be their new home.

Past photos of last Halloween when she dressed as a slutty cat — or, at least, that's what her caption says. She has whiskers painted on her cheeks and wears a black leotard.

I sigh. Lean back.

This is taking too long.

I need to be in the kitchen. I need to support my daughter. I need to be the dad I'm promising I'll be.

I glance at the clock. I'll keep looking for another two minutes, then I'll give up.

I come across photos from last summer. She wears a red, frilly skirt and holds a cat, smiling at the camera with her tongue poking out, like it's too big for her mouth, and I hate this girl. I don't just resent her for what she's done, but for who she is, and who she tries to be. She is everything I despise in a person. Self-obsessed, inward thinking, and lives her entire life on social media.

I know she's just a girl, and this is what most teenagers are like — but that's the problem. She isn't just a one-off, and maybe that's what I despise the most. That she is a single person who is representative of a larger portion of people.

Another glance at the clock tells me it's time to give up. Go support Harper. Be there for her for once.

I do a last few scrolls.

Then, just as I get ready to shut down the computer, I see it.

Destiny. The arm. The photo

The caption *me & my dad.*

And my entire body stiffs, and I am unable to help myself whispering, "Oh dear God."

[49]

HARPER

As Felix scrolls through my messages, he doesn't stop to read them.

Not a single one.

It's like he's checking something. As if he's making sure they are all there.

But he's not reading them.

Why isn't he reading them?

I watch the screen as he begins highlighting every single message.

"What are you doing?" I ask.

"Tell me more about the threats," he says, ignoring my question; though it doesn't seem like he cares. "At what point did they say you should kill your father?"

"It wasn't really said, just... I don't know. If you look at the messages..."

But he's not looking at them. He's continuing to highlight them.

"And why did you not kill him?" he asks.

"Because he's my father. I wouldn't kill him."

"But you were so close."

"Not really."

"You said you would do it."

"Yes, but I never would have. It was just a moment. I wouldn't have actually followed through."

"So this person was just wasting your time, then?"

It's a strange question.

Wasting my time?

He was grooming me. Manipulating me. Manoeuvring me into a position where I could join this supposed Death Club. Why would my refusal be wasting his time?

I look at the door, wishing Dad would walk through it. Where is he?

"Even after he said he believed in you," Felix adds.

"What?"

"After he believed you could do it, why didn't you?"

I look into his eyes, and see nothing of kindness, nothing of understanding; only irritation.

And it occurs to me...

I never told him that Danny said he believed in me.

"I don't know," I say, and feel my arms begin to tremble.

I glance at the door again.

Come on, Dad.

Please.

"But you had the knife in your hand?"

"I guess so."

He shakes his head.

"Coward," he adds.

My breath catches in my throat.

I want Dad.

"I'm just going to find my dad," I say.

I go to get up, but he slams his fist on the table, hard.

"Sit down," he says, cold and blank and forceful.

I do as he says.

And I watch the screen of his computer as he finishes highlighting every message.

"It's pathetic little girls like you," he says, "that cause people like me such stress. You and your silly little messages."

And I watch his finger as he hits delete.

Every message disappears from the screen.

Every piece of evidence gone.

And Dad is still in the other room.

[50]

WILL

It can't be.

There must be some mistake.

Her surname is *Hill,* not *Felix.*

But she said it...

Her parents divorced. She took her mother's maiden name.

And now the father of a psychotic girl is in the kitchen with my daughter.

I shut down the computer. Stand. Walk slowly and robotically through the hallway, every step an omen.

I enter the kitchen.

Harper stares at me. There is fear in her eyes. She is terrified.

She knows.

Felix turns to me and grins.

"Will," he says. "Why don't you take a seat. We were just going through what happened."

"I think you should—"

"Take a seat, Will."

I do not disobey. I take a seat beside my daughter.

"No," Felix says. "Over here."

He indicates the seat across the table from Harper. As far away from her as a seat at the table would allow.

I want to grab a knife.

I want to slam the computer against his head and tell Harper to run.

I want to be brave and fight him and save my daughter.

As it is, I do what we all know I will do, and sit in the seat I'm told to sit in.

"Harper was just telling me about how she was going to kill you," he announces. "Why don't you tell him more?"

Harper's eyes widen. They look into mine.

She is a little girl again.

Terrified.

Alone.

No, not alone. Not anymore.

"Tell him, Harper."

She says nothing. Just stares at me.

"It's okay," I tell her. "You don't have to tell me anything."

Felix slams his fist on the table and it makes both of us jump.

"I'm giving the instructions here."

I look at his belt. CS spray. Baton. Handcuffs. And rope, which seems unusual.

Is he even a real police officer?

"Harper, tell him."

"Danny tried to get me to kill you, Dad."

"And you almost did, didn't you?"

She says nothing.

I don't need her to. I will support her. I will not let him manipulate us.

"It wasn't Destiny, was it?" I ask.

"I beg your pardon?" he replies with a ruthless politeness that makes me want to shut up.

But it's shutting up that's caused so many problems for me already.

"It was you. You were sending the messages."

"You were abusing my daughter."

I chuckle. I don't know why. It just comes out. Perhaps it's the irony of an abuser calling me an abuser.

I'm beginning to see where Destiny gets her delusions from.

"She would come home every night and cry because of you," he tells me. "For months, I've had to hear her down the phone, in tears, because of *you*."

"Months? She only started this last week."

"*Enough!* No more lies!"

I go to object, to tell him I'm not lying, but it would be pointless. I couldn't reason with Destiny, and I can't reason with him. My priority is my daughter. I need to do what I can to keep her safe. Above all else, I need to ensure she's safe.

I look at her. My girl. My daughter. My world.

My failure.

"Harper," I say, quietly, even though he'll hear every word. "Listen to me."

"Enough!"

I ignore him.

"In a moment, I want you to run. Out of the house, to one of the neighbours, and get them to call 999."

"I said enough!"

"Do not worry about me. Just get help, and get yourself to safety."

She nods. A tear runs down her cheek, and I wish I could wipe it away.

"It'll be okay," I assure her.

"Stop it."

"It will—"

Felix grabs Harper by the back of the hair and in such a quick movement it doesn't register at first, he slams her head against the table.

"No!" I shout, and he goes to do it again.

I dive on him.

He shoves me off, and keeps hold of Harper.

I've never been in a fight in my life. I've never swung a punch, and I've never taken one. I have no idea what I'm doing, but I don't have a choice — I leap toward the arm that holds Harper and bite it, digging my teeth in, hard, feeling his flesh and bone.

He releases Harper and she falls to the floor. Dizzy. Groggy.

Come on Harper, please get up. Please battle through it.

Felix punches my chin and knocks me off. The pain overwhelms me to begin with, then subsides. The adrenaline makes it tolerable, if only temporarily.

He reaches for Harper again and I dive on his back, wrapping my arms around his neck.

"Go, Harper! Go!"

She pushes herself to her feet and stumbles. She's concussed and, under other circumstances, I would be calling an ambulance — but I need her to get help.

"Come on!"

Finally, she gathers herself, and stares at us.

Felix is too strong for me. He lunges an elbow backwards, into my chest, winding me, taking me to the floor, then launches his head forward and headbutts me.

My grip loosens and I feel blood trickle from my nose and land on my lip.

Harper runs.

Felix goes after her, but I push myself up, dive, and manage to grab a foot and trip him up.

His hand just misses Harper, and she is able to make it to the door, and leave, running into the storm.

Felix doesn't go after her.

He stands. Towering over me as I lay on the floor, staring up at his intimidating presence.

He smirks.

He can smile all he wants, Harper made it out.

He crouches over me. His grin widens.

"You idiot," he tells me.

I say nothing.

He can call me an idiot all he wants, anything that stalls him, anything that bides time while we wait for the real police to get here.

But he doesn't seem bothered. In fact, he laughs; a slow, ominous chuckle.

"Really, I never get guys like you. Supposed to be smart but as stupid as it comes."

That's it, keep talking.

Keep wasting time.

"Do you really think I came alone?"

This throws me. "What?"

"Do you really think there's no one else out there?"

I don't understand what he means at first, then I realise; Destiny. She's still out there.

Harper will be running straight toward her.

I try to push myself to my feet, but a boot in my face forces me back to the floor. I'm too dizzy to fight, meaning it's easy for him to mount my back and pull my hands behind me.

"Harper!" I shout. "Harper!"

But it's no good. She's in the middle of the storm and all she'll be able to hear is rain.

The discomfort of steel around my wrists tells me it's over. He's handcuffed me, and I'm going nowhere.

[51]

HARPER

THE RAIN IS GETTING COLDER AND HARDER, BUT I
ignore it. It's not important. Once I get to a neighbour, I can
call the police and they can help Dad.

If they get there in time, that is.

I skid on the slippery surface of the driveway and
collapse into a puddle. The knees of my jeans rip and a
patch of blood accompanies a slight sting, but I push myself
up again. I can deal with it later.

I'm not a good runner. I've never tried hard in PE or
been into sports, but I run hard now, sprinting, trying to
make it to the end of the drive.

But I don't.

I halt.

A silhouette watches me. Familiar. Standing at the end
of the drive, blocking my escape. I squint to see who it is.

She steps forward and her face emerges and it's her, it's
her, she's still here — what is she still doing here?

I almost turn to run back into the house, but it's just as
bad in there as it is out here, then I consider if I can run past

her, but I can't, she's tall, athletic, crazy, she'll get me, she'll stop me oh God oh God she'll stop me.

"Harper," she says, shouting to be heard above the elements.

That's all she says.

She's calling out to me, like she wants to talk.

I don't move.

"Harper, I need to tell you the truth."

I glance over my shoulder.

The front door is still open.

What if Felix has killed Dad? What if he comes running after me?

I'm not sure Dad even knows how to handle himself. Felix is a big guy. Dad's a scrawny, tired man who lets his alcoholic wife walk all over him.

"I want to tell you the truth about your Dad," she says.

"Go away!"

I hate myself for the tremble in my voice.

"But I have to tell you the truth."

"Just leave me alone!"

I don't care what she says; all I care about is getting past her, getting across the drive, away from the house, and to a neighbour.

But as she steps toward me, I step back, and a puddle makes me slip, and I try to get up but my legs are heavy and I can't.

She stands over me. Her face becomes clearer. She looks like any other insecure teenage girl, but I find it hard to see anything but a monster.

"Don't believe his lies, Harper."

"Please, just let me go."

She crouches over me. Rain hits her face as furiously as it hits mine, but while water drips from my hair into my eyes and I have to wipe it away to be able to see, she doesn't seem at all bothered.

"Is there really no way I can convince you?" she asks.

"No. There isn't."

"Oh, Harper. Then I have no reason to keep you."

I push myself to my feet and go to run but her hand is around my ankle and I fall on my face, hard, hard against the ground, and my elbows scrape and my knees scrape and I see blood.

Her foot presses into my back. She's wearing heels.

Her hand grabs my hair, lifts my head, exposes my neck, and I wait for a knife to meet my skin but it doesn't. I don't even know if she has a weapon. I just expect it.

"I loved your dad, Harper," she says, leaning down, putting her lips as close to my ear as I can.

The feel of her breath makes me shiver.

"But he hurt me. And now I have to hurt him."

"Please..."

Something metal clamps around my wrist, then the other. My hands are bound behind my back. I try to push myself up with my legs but I can't balance.

She's laughing.

I can hear her laughing.

Yet, as I look at her, watching the rain wash away her makeup, ruining her outfit, causing the hair dye to run down her neck, I realise she is nothing but evil without its disguise.

And I see you, Destiny.

I see what you are.

"You're pathetic," I tell her.

She giggles. Like a little girl.

"You really are."

"Me? Look at you!"

"You are—"

"You have no friends. No family. You are so fucking lonely you let a stranger on the internet turn you into a liar. You are pathetic, Harper. You are."

"I know."

She laughs.

"I know I'm pathetic," I continue. "But at least I'm aware. You walk around clueless, believing you're perfect, with no idea just how much everyone hates you. At least I know everyone detests me — do you?"

Her smiles and her laughs subside, replaced by a sneer, a vile flicker of anger.

She leans down, close to me, our lips almost touching, my eyes losing focus, and I can smell the mint chewing gum and the cheap perfume mixed with rainwater.

"Talk to me like that again," she says, "and I will kill you before Daddy gets the chance."

I almost think she's going to kiss me. She's unstable enough. Instead, she stands, grabs me by the hair, lifts me to my feet, and she drags me across the drive and into the house and through to the dining room where she shoves me onto a chair.

Next to Dad.

Who is also handcuffed.

And Destiny stands next to her father — *her daddy* — and they look at their catch, admiring their work, and I wonder if we're about to die.

[52]

WILL

I was holding onto the only hope I had — that Harper made it out alive. The only way to endure this sick bastard's tirade is knowing that my daughter made it out alive, and that she is safe.

But the door opens, and here she is.

A drenched Destiny enters, dragging Harper by the hair, and my world ends.

I can't even move, can't even reach a hand out to her, as it is fastened around the back my seat. I try to reach out to her with my eyes, try to show her I love her, but she can't look up. I don't know if it's shame or terror — or both — but she can't even lift her face.

Destiny joins her demented father and they stand before us, looking at us with such satisfaction, such smug faces, pleased that they've won.

"Go get a knife, darling," says Felix, and Destiny obliges, sauntering into the kitchen, swaying her backside from side to side, collecting a knife and practically dancing back into the room. Her jauntiness is terrifying.

Felix steps toward me. Stands over me. Casts me in his shadow. Leers.

"Do you regret it?" he asks, and I have no idea what he's talking about.

I look at Harper, trying to catch her eye. Maybe if I kick up enough of a fuss, she can make a run for it.

Felix's fist lands on my chin, sending pain rushing up the side of my neck and my face.

"I'm talking to you."

Despite my better judgement, the coward in me prevails, and I look at up at him.

"I said, do you regret it?"

"Regret what?" I spit.

Felix laughs. Looks at Destiny, who folds her arms. Shakes her head pitifully, her disdain directed at me.

He punches me again, this time in my belly. It winds me, it's a while before I can breathe properly again.

"Answer the question," he says.

"I would if I knew what you were talking about."

I'd love to say that this was a witty retort, a defiance in the face of danger — but it was genuine pleading. I want to know what he's asking me so I can answer it and prevent further pain.

"You..." Felix's anger becomes too much and he strikes me again, this time in the side of my neck, and for a few seconds I can't breathe, and I panic until I'm able to take in air again.

"Do you regret it?"

"Regret what?"

I hate the desperation in my voice.

"Leading me on!" Destiny interjects, her voice shrill and unhinged. "For making me think you love me! For hurting a girl as young as me!"

I'd laugh if this wasn't so frightening. They are both as sick and deluded as each other.

"I didn't."

"What did you say?" Felix grips my neck.

"I said... I didn't."

"Are you accusing my daughter of lying?"

I glance at Destiny, who looks to be taking much satisfaction from my pain.

I try to reply, but his grip is too tight. He loosens it so I can talk.

"I don't think she's lying," I answer. "Just mistaken."

"Mistaken?"

"She's convinced I love her, and she believes it, so she's not lying. But that still doesn't mean it's true."

Felix turns to his daughter, they exchange a look of disbelief, and he bursts into raucous laughter.

"Well what do you know! He sounds like a fucking teacher, through and through, doesn't he?"

"Please..."

I look at Harper. Her head has dropped. She's crying silently, and I feel angry and scared and vengeful and hopeless all at the same time.

"You being smart with me?" Felix asks.

"No..."

"You think you're better than me, that you're a good talker, that it?"

"No, I just..."

"Just what?" He gets close to me again. "What? What is it you want?"

"For you to leave us alone. Please, and we will leave you alone too."

"Oh, it's too late for that." He looks over his shoulder at Destiny. "Wouldn't you say, dearest?"

"Oh, far, far too late," she concurs.

Felix steps away and walks up to his daughter, placing a hand on her face. He kisses her forehead and she smiles dotingly and I hate that, despite being a sick bastard, this guy is still a better father than me.

"Who wouldn't want a girl like this?" he asks me. "Do you know what I think?"

He doesn't wait for a reply.

"I think any man of your age would want this beautiful young woman. You were lucky enough that she gave a little interest your way, and you took advantage."

"That's not what happened—"

"Stop lying!" he screams.

He takes a moment, allows his heavy breathing to subside, and once he is calm enough, he takes the hand of his daughter.

"My darling," he says, "which would you like?"

Destiny looks satisfied with this question, and she shifts her seductive gaze between me and Harper, back to me, back to Harper, back to me, then back to Harper.

"Her," she decides. "I want to kill her."

Harper lifts her head.

"No," I say. "No! You can't! Have me instead!"

Felix chuckles. "You don't get it, there's no *instead* — just which of you I kill, and which of you my dearest kills."

"No... Please... I'll do anything..."

"Anything? How about turn back time and avoid breaking my daughter's heart, hey? How about not taking advantage of her!"

I go to respond, but I can't reason with them. I've tried. Death is inevitable.

"Fine," I say, taking a different tact. "Fine, I hurt her. I took advantage. Is that what you want? It was my fault, I take responsibility, it was me! Now will you let my daughter go?"

"Finally!" Felix gesticulates wildly to emphasise his glee. "Bloody finally! He admits it — glory hallelujah!"

"Now will you let her go?"

His grin widens.

"Darling," he says, turning toward his daughter and handing her some rope. "Why don't you take Harper upstairs for a little girl time?"

"Oh, yes Daddy, yes!"

Destiny dances over to Harper and grabs her by the hair.

"No!" I scream, and I do everything I can to try to stand up. "No! Leave her alone! Leave her alone!"

Harper struggles, but Destiny puts a knife by her throat and she stops.

"Don't hurt her! Leave her alone!"

I manage to stand, but the chair that's still bound to my back becomes too heavy and I fall. Nevertheless, I force myself back to my feet, struggling to balance.

Felix gives Destiny some rope as she drags Harper out of the room and up the stairs.

I try to chase after, but a fist in the side of my head knocks me to the ground, and everything loses focus.

[53]

HARPER

Destiny drags me to my room and throws me onto my bed. I try to get up, and I try to struggle, but the hand-cuffs are so tight that all movement causes pain.

She pushes me onto my back and sits on top of me. Her perfect legs are either side of my waist, and her dress rides up to the base of her underwear. Everything about her is sexual, from the way she moves, to the way she sits on top of me, to the way she reveals everything without being obviously obscene. Even the way she smiles is erotic. Her tongue presses playfully against the gap between her top and bottom teeth — and it strikes me just how different we are.

Destiny likes to be noticed. She likes boys to look at her. She likes to sit at the centre of the lunch table and have people laugh. I prefer to sink into the background. I prefer to enter a room and leave it later without anyone ever knowing I was there.

Maybe it won't be too bad if I die. There won't be a gap in anyone's life, there wouldn't be a tree planted for me at school, and there wouldn't be anyone who would remember my name in a year's time.

But then there's Dad.

I'm finally getting a father.

And that's something I do want to live for.

"Oh, Harper," Destiny says in a singsong voice normally reserved for toddlers. She giggles, and it comes out like a squeak, and my entire body fills with contempt.

"What are we going to do with you?" She pretends to think. "First, let's get you tied up."

She uses her rope to tie my ankles to the corners of the bed, tying them hard. I try to resist but she places the tip of the knife against my throat and says, "Struggle, and it all ends here," then finishes tying my ankle and takes out a key.

She keeps the knife by my neck, tells me to sit up, uses her spare hand to release one of my wrists from the handcuffs. She lies me back down and lifts the still cuffed wrist to the railing headboard at the top of my bed.

She goes to move my other hand, but I keep it behind my back.

She smirks.

"Try it," she tells me. She presses the knife harder against my neck, and she lowers her face to mine. "Try it and they won't even have a face for someone to identify."

I allow her to take my hand.

"There we go!" she says, full of cheer again.

She puts the handcuff back around my wrist, binding me to the headboard.

She sits up again and rests her hands on my belly, making me feel stupid and pathetic, and she seems to enjoy it.

"Are you worried about your dad?" she asks me.

I don't answer, which she takes as a yes.

"I promise he'll die quickly. As long as he doesn't struggle too much, that is..."

She stands. Wanders around my room, running her hand over my compact mirror, over the draws of my cupboard, looking at the posters on my wall.

"And what about me?" I ask her. "Am I going to die quickly?"

She turns back to me with what appears to be a renewed sense of excitement.

Is this turning her on? Thrilling her? Does she find my torment exhilarating? There is so much wrong with this girl. With her and her dad. I'd feel sorry for her if she wasn't so terrifying.

"Oh, eventually," she says, casually. "I mean, once I get round to it."

"And until then?"

"Just thought we could hang out, you know? Like girl-friends."

"I'm not your friend."

"Of course not. You don't have friends." She sighs. "Yes, you're right, I guess I better not delay it too much."

She looks me dead in the eyes.

"I promise not to torture you," she says, then runs her hand up my leg and adds, "once you can't scream anymore, that is."

[54]

WILL

"She's sweet, isn't she?"

My eyes open. I must have been out for seconds.

My cheek is on the floor, with my body still bound to the chair that sticks up in the air. Felix's large black shoes pause a few feet from my face.

"Destiny, I mean. Kind of a nutjob, but sweet. Passionate. Loyal. And a real knockout — I mean, did you see her?"

He makes a *phwoar* sound.

"I mean, whoever takes her to her prom — assuming they have one at her school, since it's more of an American thing and all that — well, they are going to have a good staring down from me."

He grabs my hair and lifts me up until I'm upright in the chair again. I get a headrush, then his smug face comes into focus a few inches from mine.

"I don't like her going out with boys. I imagine you'd understand, if your daughter every actually went out with any."

He takes a few steps back and removes his belt, placing it on the side table next to the sofa. He unbuttons the top few buttons of his shirt then untucks it, waving it, trying to cool himself down.

"Are you even a real police officer?" I ask.

He chuckles. "For an educated man, you're a right idiot."

He rolls his sleeves up. First the left, then the right. His forearms are covered in tattoos of skulls and snakes. I think I may even spot a swastika there too.

"Are you proud of your daughter, Will?" he asks me, leaning on the arm of the sofa and crossing his arms thoughtfully.

I don't answer; all I can think about is getting to her, getting up those stairs and saving Harper from that teenage monster, that vile child who is doing god-knows-what to her.

"I don't know if I am, to be honest," Will tells me. "She's kind of annoying. Needy. Always floating around, asking me stupid questions. Does yours do that?"

I afford him a glance, then look back to the open door that leads to the stairs, trying to figure out how I can get up there.

Could I break this chair?

Could I break my hand and pull it out of the cuff?

Then again, what if I did get out of these restraints — do I really think I could get past Felix?

He is not only bigger than me, but tougher.

Even so, the adrenaline is running. This is my daughter's life on the line, and I'm willing to do anything.

"I divorced her mum and was pleased to get away from her, but also chuffed I only had to deal with Destiny on weekends, you know?"

I sigh.

"Felix, please—" I try, but he just talks over me.

"It's ego, I guess. I don't like anyone touching her. Especially some middle-age prick like you."

"Look, I never touched her, I never—"

"So you never kissed her?"

"*She* kissed me."

"Ah, yes, of course. A stunner like that would kiss some gangly nonce like you?"

I bow my head. This is wasting time. I need to get to Harper.

"What's the matter, Will? Don't like the truth?"

"I promise you, I don't want anything to do with your daughter."

"Why not? Don't you think she's pretty?"

"I think she's a child! I don't care about her! I don't want anything to do with her!"

"Oh, Will, let's stop the lies..."

"Please, I don't care anymore, just let Harper go. Kill me, just let her go."

Felix steps toward me, bows down, looks me in the eyes, and says, "No," before guffawing at the hilarity of such a grave situation.

I have to save her.

I have to actually be a dad for once.

Yet, as I look at this maniac fetching a knife from the kitchen, I begin to accept that it's not going to happen.

And I hate myself even more for it.

He places the tip of the knife against my throat, then holds his hand back and pretends to swing, like he's adjusting his aim, like he's getting ready to plunge it into my neck.

"You don't have to do this."

I don't know why I'm begging, he's not going to stop,

he's not going to change his mind, we're both going to die, there's nothing we can do...

"Right," he says, and holds the knife out, ready to gather plenty of momentum when he swipes it.

I shake my head.

I try begging again but the words escape me.

He swings the knife.

[55]

HARPER

Destiny wanders around the room with her hands behind her back, the knife dangling loosely between her fingers. She drags her gaze across everything, sinisterly inquisitive, scrutinising every object.

She notices a poster on my wall of my favourite band, Bullet For a Valentine. She looks at it and laughs.

"Oh my God, is this a band?" she asks. "It looks like a bunch of Satanists. Do you actually listen to their music?"

I don't reply.

"Isn't it all screamy and stuff?" She turns to me and sticks her lip out. "Does little Harper like the loud music because it makes her feel better? When someone else is angry, is it okay if you're angry?"

She giggles and turns back to the wall, strolling past the poster and reaching my desk. My teddy sits on it.

Destiny picks it up and glares into its eyes, then turns to me and laughs again.

"This your bear?"

She digs her long, painted nails into its neck and begins to rip.

"No, please don't!"

"What, you think it's real?"

"No, it's just my..."

I don't know what to tell her.

Mum bought it for me back when she still cared. That bear reminds me of when we were a happy family; it conjures images of days by the sea and nights on the sofa. It's nostalgia, in the form of a meaningless toy.

She digs her nails in, rips its head off and discards it on the floor.

"Whoops," she says.

I like to think that, if I weren't tied up, I would react to her taunts, maybe even hit her. As it is, all I can do is stare at her as she continues wandering and reaches my chest of drawers, where she notices something and reacts with shocked laughter.

"Oh my God!" she says, and the laughter becomes bigger until it's uncontrollable.

She picks up a photo frame with Danny's photo inside and shows it to me.

"You actually framed this?"

Her laughter takes her to her knees. She pounds the floor as her hilarity takes over, tears of delight falling down her cheeks, until it subsides enough that she can stand again.

"We just found this picture on Google images!" she tells me. "Seriously, we just searched for good looking young guy and took the first picture that came up. I can't believe you actually framed it!"

She wipes her eyes and tries to contain another burst of laughter.

"And I can't believe you actually sent pictures back," she tells me, placing the photo frame back on the cupboard.

"I mean, have you seen your body? To actually have the guts to send me a picture of it... If that was my body, I'd wear an anorak everywhere I go."

She approaches the end of the bed, places her hands on my ankles, and begins to crawl along the duvet.

"Just so you know, that image is everywhere now," she tells me. "I mean, not revenge porn websites or anything, you have to actually be hot to be in there... I mean mostly funny sites and stuff. People can do with a good laugh."

She crawls further up my legs until her hands reach the base of my skirt. That is where she pauses, pressing down against my legs. She is stronger than she looks, but I try not to whimper. The more I give in to the pain, the more she'll do it.

"And, by the way, I could so tell you were breathing in the whole time. Pathetic..."

She tightens her grip around my legs and it hurts, but I don't give in.

Then she produces the knife and asks me, "Where would you like me to cut first?"

Then her grinning face lowers its gaze to my skirt, and I can't help but scream.

[56]
WILL

Harper screams.

"No," I whisper.

I can't let her die.

And, in the split second between Felix swinging the knife and plunging it into in my throat, I throw myself and the chair to the floor, landing on my face.

Felix stumbles, his knife swiping through air, and his legs are off balance. I react instinctively. His ankle is by my mouth, so I reach out and clamp my teeth around it, sinking into the flesh.

He screams and lunges the knife downwards.

I move my back so the chair blocks his strike, knocking the knife out of his hand and sending it flying across the room.

Like everything in this house, the chair I'm attached to is old and weak, meaning that, in a quick movement, I am able to throw myself onto my back and smash it. My hands remain fastened behind my back, but I no longer have the chair to contend with.

I lunge myself at his throat. His eyes widen, but I am

quicker than he expects, and I land my teeth in his neck before he can stop me.

I bite down hard, then harder still. My knowledge of science is limited, but I've covered enough biology lessons to know that his jugular veins are located at the side of his neck. The carotid arteries are also close by. Once my teeth penetrate them, rapid haemorrhaging will start, and I just have to hang on for dear life for as long as it takes for him to die.

The adrenaline flows makes my body shake, and I close my eyes and just focus on keeping my teeth in place, ignoring how much he fights back.

The blood doesn't just dribble, but flows down my chin. It's sticky and thick, and I know I have the right place; I just have to hang on.

For as long as it takes, however much he fights, however much he thrashes.

He lifts me and shoves me against the wall, pulling me back and barging me against it again, and again, causing pain to shoot up and down my spine.

Then his fists start.

At first, into my rib cage, a few times, then against my skull, again and again, and it makes me go dizzy but I force my eyes to stay open, widening them to ensure he does not knock me out, and I do not lose consciousness.

He even tries grabbing my hair and pulling my head away, but that just hurts him more as I keep my teeth dug in.

His actions become weaker, and he tries to scream, but it just comes out in gargles. He doesn't lose resolve, but he loses strength.

In a last act of desperation, his hand wraps around my

scrotum, squeezes, harder, and pulls — but it doesn't do much, as his arm falls limp shortly after he starts.

His body gives up.

I feel his arms vaguely tapping me, his last few movements, then they flop.

And, even though he doesn't move, I know he could be faking, or be unconscious, so I don't stop. I continue biting down, not releasing my jaw until the time has passed and I am certain.

When I do release my mouth from his neck, it takes a while for the ache to lessen.

I look down. Not just sprinkles, but douses of blood stick to my clothes. Some of it glows as lightning flashes outside the window.

I don't allow myself long to recuperate, but I give myself a moment, allowing my panting to subside. I spit out any blood that remains in my mouth, and I try not to think about what I've just done.

A dead body lies next to me; one I've created. It's a bizarre feeling, a mixture of terror, self-realisation and relief.

But it doesn't last long.

I see the piece of silver that will release me left beside the CS spray and baton. I grab it and remove my handcuffs as quick my dizziness will allow me.

[57]

HARPER

DESTINY RESTS THE KNIFE AGAINST MY KNEE AND begins to drag it, slowly upwards, producing a small line of blood as she does.

It stings more than hurts, and I try not to wince but I can feel my tears accumulating.

She lifts my skirt with the knife, a long line of blood meeting the base of my underwear.

She cackles. Another burst of uncontrollable laughter follows as she points at my large, black knickers, and the pubic hair that protrudes from them.

"You have got to be kidding me!" she says. "Look at that hairy mound! Granny knickers and no bikini wax? You really never wanted a boy to notice you, did you?"

The knife still rests besides the tufts of coarse black hair, and she presses the tip against it, only slightly, but enough to make me cry.

"Please..." I say. "Please, I've done nothing to you..."

"Done nothing to me? Do you not know what your father did?"

"That was my dad, not me!"

She presses the knife further into my skin and I feel the blood trickling down the inside of my thigh.

"How far does the apple fall from the tree though, Harper?"

"Please..."

"After all, you were prepared to kill him only hours ago, were you not?"

"Please don't..."

"And think, if you'd have done it, you'd have saved both you and him from this. You are a silly, silly girl..."

She drags the knife further upwards, slicing into the base of my underwear, cutting it open, then dragging the knife to my waist. Blood sinks into the matted curls, and she still laughs. It doesn't stop.

It's constant.

Girlish giggling, so sweet and innocent, like she is playing with Barbies.

And I stare at her, and I see her. Beneath that smile, that psychotic demeanour, is something else. Something scared, something hidden.

"Your dad really messed you up, didn't he?" I say.

"Excuse me?" she says, raising an eyebrow, grinning at my stupidity.

"It's okay, you know," I tell her. "My dad messed me up too."

"Please, my dad is the best—"

"I bet they split up, didn't they?"

Her smile fades for a moment, then she forces it back to her lips.

"It sucks, doesn't it? Knowing that they were perfectly happy before you came along."

She digs the knife in harder, and the blood comes out thicker and more and more of it dribbles down my thighs.

But I'm onto something.

I know it.

So I don't stop.

"I've laid in this bed wishing he would come and ask me how I was, or what happened in my day, every night for the past few years. Have you done that?"

"I live with my mum—"

"Yeah, but I bet he never even picks up the phone, does he?"

She pushes harder and I scream, but it doesn't deter me.

"You think he's doing this for you?" I say. "You think he's taking revenge on my dad for you? It's for his own pride that someone else managed to screw up his daughter for him."

She takes the knife out and swipes it down, reaching the top of my leg, and more blood dribbles down me, but I ignore it.

Suddenly, I'm a little less scared.

And, bizarrely, I hate her a little less.

In fact, I look at her and I don't see the dyed hair, the dress, the nails...

I see *me*.

And I see what her pain has driven her to.

"That's why you're obsessed isn't it?" I say. "With my dad? Because you needed a father figure, and all you had was abuse."

"My dad loves me!"

"Your dad thinks you're a tart! Your dad only cares about his own ego, and the damage someone touching his daughter will do to it. He cares for you as much as he cares for a stray cat he picks up and kicks around for fun."

"I'm warning you!"

"No matter what you do, there's nothing you can do to make him actually love you."

"He does love me!"

"Love you? Destiny, he doesn't even *like* you."

She lifts the knife from my crotch to my neck, and I can see it in her eyes — this is the end, this is the moment her temper overtakes her and this is the moment I've pushed her too far.

Then she hears a noise. A clatter on the stairs. A stumble.

"What was that?" she whispers, and she takes her knife and goes to the door.

[58]

WILL

Once freed, I don't wait around to feel the relief of freedom or the release of pain; I leap to my feet, full of fury, and charge to the stairs so hard that I stumble over the first few and knock against the wall.

The door to Harper's room opens and Destiny appears at the top of the stairs. She grins at me. Mocks my desperation. Waves the knife around like a cigarette.

I stampede up the stairs, taking them two at a time, and when I swing my fist and it lands in the side of her head, I'm almost as startled as she is, but it doesn't last long; my focus is on the knife.

She falls to her knees. I take hold of her wrist in one hand and squeeze against the bone. It feels so fragile, like a child's wrist, like I could snap it if I knew how. But I don't. I just squeeze until her grip loosens and I take her knife from her.

Inside the room I see her. My daughter. Fixed to the bed. Her skirt lifted over her belly and a line of blood trickling onto the bedsheets.

"Dad..." she whispers.

My anger takes over, and I don't care what happens to Destiny, I don't care what I do to her, I just want her gone; whether by her choice or by a body bag.

But I'm still dizzy, still weak, and all it takes is Destiny to barge into my waist and, despite the lesser strength her age and gender has given her, I tumble down the stairs, knocking my neck against a step and my spine against the wall, until I land at the bottom and the knife tumbles out of my hand.

I lift my head and wait for everything to return to focus while Destiny returns to Harper's bedroom and the door closes.

I stumble to my knees. There is a pain in my neck. An aching in the base of my back and up my spine. My knees feel tender.

I struggle to my feet and fall back down again, just avoiding the knife on the floor, panting, wiping blood from my sleeve, unsure whether it's mine or hers. I force myself to stand, catching sight of Felix as I do. In the living room. An empty body. Vacant of life. Unable to hurt anyone else.

I did that, I remind myself.

I did that, and I am stronger than I think.

If I can defeat a big guy like that, then a teenage girl should be nothing.

I take the knife and use the bannister to balance my body. I stand, for a moment, swaying from side to side, waiting for the headrush to leave. My head is pounding, and I know I'm concussed or something like it, and in dire need of a hospital, but I can drop down dead for all I care; so long as I make sure Harper is safe first.

I'm lucky, really. Some people die falling down the stairs. I just have a headache and a few pains.

That's all they are.

Just a headache. Just a few pains.

Even though they are far, far worse, that's what I have to tell myself; just a headache. Just a few pains.

Minimise it.

Shrink the agony to a tiny little twinge, and that's all it will be.

I try the first few steps. I'm swaying from side to side, but I'm staying upright, and that's the main thing.

[59]

HARPER

Dad's fall down the stairs is followed by silence, and Destiny returns to the room with even more smugness — if that's possible.

She shuts the door. Drags my chair across the room and wedges it against the door handle. Turns to me and shrugs sympathetically.

"Looks like we're out of time," she says, and then she's on the bed and she's on me and her hands are around my throat and her thumbs dig into my windpipe, and she knows where to press to stop the air, it's like she's done this before. Her face changes. It contorts, fading from one visage of rage to another, her smiles and chuckles and smugness have changed into the fury she needs to kill me.

I stare up at her, struggling, pulling on my handcuffs, pulling on the rope around my ankles, feeling more and more helpless.

I still have to fight. I have to try.

But the fight starts to leave me.

I weaken.

The world begins to fade.

My body stops struggling, stops battling.

But I can hear something. The door. Distant, like it's far away. A banging against it.

Destiny presses down harder, like she wants to speed up my death.

The banging continues, then the door bursts open and Dad runs in and knocks Destiny off me and I suck in air, suck it in, breathe and breathe and breathe and turn my head to see Destiny leap to her feet; but this only presents her gut to Dad's knife.

It goes through her dress and sinks through her flesh, but Dad doesn't stop there. He pushes. Harder and harder, as the knife goes further into her body.

She looks helpless. There is a new vulnerability in the way she looks from Dad to me, then back to Dad. A fear she has yet to show either of us.

Dad doesn't stop. The knife is deep within her, yes, but it's not enough, so he twists it. Holds it in her and, with all his strength, twists it, and I don't know whether to be grateful for him or scared of him.

He pushes her against the wall beside the window, which he opens.

With a scream and a burst of strength, Dad pushes her to the window, drops the knife to open it, and she topples over the ledge, falling out of it headfirst.

Dad stands at the ledge, looking down.

He doesn't move. He stays at the window, his back to me, staring downwards. Panting. His whole body is heaving as he breathes.

Finally, he looks over his shoulder at me, and I don't know what I expect to see — a look of terror, fear, despair, happiness, I don't know...

In the end, it looks to be all of those.

He says two words that I can tell he really needs to say:
"It's over."

[60]

WILL

"It's over."

I say it again for my own sake.

"It is over."

There's guilt for the damage I've done to a young woman, but also relief, desperate relief.

Felix is dead downstairs.

And Destiny is... well, she isn't moving.

And my daughter stares at me, a mixture of tears and respite.

I rush to her side, and untie the ropes from her ankles. I left the keys to the handcuffs downstairs, but I'm reluctant to leave her.

"The keys are downstairs," I tell her. "I'll be right back, I promise, I'll be right back."

I'm terrified to leave her, scared of what could happen, so I leap down the steps three at a time, fall down the last few, then skid around the hallway and into the living room.

Felix stares at the ceiling, his body still.

I did that.

But I can't think about it now. I can deal with it later.

I take the keys and race back upstairs.

I breathe a sigh of relief; Harper is still there.

I place the keys into the lock, almost fumbling, and release her wrists.

Almost as soon as the handcuffs drop behind the bed her arms are around me, and they are hugging me so tight that, for a moment, I can't breathe.

I wrap my arms around her, and we do not let go.

My collar becomes damp as she cries into it, and she is so loud, but it's fine. It's all fine. There's blood on the bedsheets, and blood sticks to my shirt. There's pain throughout my body, and there's terror in Harper's sobs. But these are all things we can deal with later.

For now, I just hold her.

Then I whisper in her ear, "I am so proud of you."

She cries harder.

"I love you so much," I continue. "I am so proud of you. I am so, so proud. You were so strong. And I'm sorry, I'm so, so sorry."

She pulls me tighter.

"I am so sorry..."

[61]

HARPER

They are words that I've wanted to hear for so long.

I'm proud of you.

I love you.

I'm sorry.

But none of it can match the feeling of watching my father fight for me. He didn't leave me, he didn't let her hurt me, not too much anyway, he came back, and he came through.

Despite being pushed downstairs, knocked about and covered in blood, he came back for me.

That's all I've ever wanted.

I pull away for a moment. His eyes are damp too. Not as damp as mine, I'm sure, my cheeks are soaked, but there is pain in there, and there is love too.

"I'm sorry too, Dad," I tell him.

"Don't, I am the one who should be sorry."

"It wasn't your fault, that girl was crazy."

"I don't just mean that. I mean..."

He looks down.

"I know," I tell him, then I wrap my arms around him again, and I don't stop crying.

Eventually, he pulls away and says, "I need to go call the police now, okay?"

"Don't go."

"I'll be one minute, then I'll be right back, I promise."

I nod, but I still cling to his hand. He stands and backs away, and he escapes my grasp, but he doesn't stop watching me until he's out of sight.

A few seconds later, I hear his voice as he speaks down the phone.

I step away from the bed. My legs are weak. There is a pain running up the inside of my thigh, but I don't think the cut was too deep. It stings, but it doesn't stop me from limping across the room to the window.

I pause, feeling the cold air, not realising how sweaty I am.

Destiny's body lies on the drive below. Her arms and legs spread out chaotically. A pool of blood spreads from beneath her stab wound, and most of her dress is a thick red.

She turns slightly.

She's still alive.

I consider whether to tell Dad when he's back. Whether we should do something about it.

But alive or not, she's not getting up.

We're safe now.

I don't believe it, and I have to keep telling myself it, but we're safe. I'm sure of it.

Dad returns to the room and joins me at the window. Once he sees what I'm looking at, he goes to pull me away.

"No... I have to see this..."

It's ridiculous, I know, but I have to watch her. I have to make sure she doesn't get up. I have to make sure she doesn't come back. So long as she's on the drive, she can't hurt me, and I have to make sure she stays there.

Dad seems to understand. He places an arm around me, kisses my forehead, and stays with me until the police arrive.

[62]

WILL

THE SIRENS ARE DISTANT, AT FIRST, THEN THEY GROW
louder. Before I know it, they are deafening.

I go outside to greet the police and direct them inside.

An ambulance arrives next.

A paramedic comes toward me, but I tell them my
daughter's upstairs and she's more important. Another
tends to Destiny, though I don't know how much they'll be
able to do for her.

Another ambulance arrives and the paramedic insists
on seeing me, and I reluctantly oblige. I refuse to go to the
hospital though, not wanting to be away from Harper. Even
if we both go to the hospital, they might put us in separate
rooms, and I am staying wherever she is.

They fetch me some water and a few pills. They
bandage my lower back and do other stuff I don't pay attention to.

A police officer takes my statement, my record of what
happened here. He says he'll need me to come to the station
and talk more about it later.

The media arrive quicker than the police anticipated, but they manage to keep them off the drive.

Then, after a moment of silence passes, I wonder if I should ask my questions now. Despite all the police officers here, I am still worried that one of them could be lying, that they could be a fake, like Felix, and I have to remind myself that they would know if one of them wasn't their colleague.

"So who was he?" I ask.

"Simon Felix?" the police replies, as if he needs to confirm who I'm talking about.

I nod faintly.

"He wasn't lying about being a police officer, only about whether he was still in active duty. He was discharged nine months ago."

"Why?"

"The same delusions that destroyed his marriage destroyed his job. He kept imagining suspects were doing things they weren't. Then he started harassing his female colleagues."

"Really?"

"Last I heard he was trying to use his computer to hack the police database. He was a really messed up man, I'm afraid."

"You don't have to tell me."

The police officer places a hand on my shoulder.

"You protected your family," he tells me. "You did what any of us would do. Remember that. The problems he was having were not yours."

I nod. I go to say thank you, but the words don't meet my lips.

He wanders away, shouting at the media to get back. I see the flashes of their cameras reflected in the puddles, but I am out of sight in the back of this ambulance.

The paramedic applies a few finishing touches to the bandages, then turns and asks me whether my head is feeling any better. I reply, but I'm not sure what I say.

My focus is on Destiny. They have placed her on a bed and are putting her in the back of an ambulance.

I'm pretty sure I hear one of them say they are taking her to intensive care, and I wonder how she's managed to survive.

[63]

HARPER

I watch the melee of people from my bedroom window as the paramedic stitches my leg, saying every few minutes that they will need to take me in.

I tell them okay, but not yet.

First, I need to see this.

Not the media craning to get their photos, the sick vultures preying upon the wounded, their voyeurism more important than ethics.

Not the police gathering, putting up tape, talking to Dad.

Not even the coroner taking out Felix's body.

It's Destiny I'm interested in. The fear that she will get up at any moment still grips me.

The paramedics gather around her. They press their hands against her stab wound, trying to stop the bleeding.

When she's ready, they lift her onto the stretcher and take her to the ambulance.

Just before she goes in, her eyes open.

They lock onto mine, if only for a few seconds.

And, at the very moment she disappears into the vehicle, I am sure I see her smile.

A small, sinister smile.

A tiny act of malice.

And one I am sure was intended for me.

THREE WEEKS LATER

[64]

WILL

ANOTHER DAY OF TEACHING ENDS AND I AM
exhausted.

But it's a good kind of exhaustion.

I've been on my feet all day, delivering lessons I spent
Sunday afternoon designing, full of activities where my
class is moving around, interacting, and engaging in their
learning. The monotonous procedure of lecturing through a
mock paper is a distant memory.

The students even say goodbye to me when they
leave my classroom. It's a small action, and it's bizarre
that it means so much, yet it's something I haven't had for
years — where, instead of shuffling out with their heads
down, they smile at me and tell me to have a good
afternoon.

One girl even says thank you. It feels strange yet
brilliant.

When I arrive home with a box of books, Harper is in
the kitchen. I hear sizzling from a frying pan and I am
greeted with the most pleasant of aromas.

"Oh wow," I say. "What are we having?"

I walk up to her and give her a hug with my spare arm, then place my box out of the way.

"Bacon, sausages and eggs."

"Sounds perfect."

She serves our tea and we sit opposite each other, eating whilst in eager conversation. I ask her about her day and she tells me about her science lesson where they were dissecting pig hearts. It sounds gross, but the experiment isn't what she focusses on — it's the new girl she was paired with, and how she was able to have a laugh with her.

I've never heard her talk about having a laugh with another girl before. I ask what this girl's name is, and she tell me it's Hope.

"Maybe you should invite Hope around," I tell her. "Or go to the cinema with her at the weekend or something."

"Maybe," she replies, not in a dismissive way, but with actual thought given to it.

She asks me how my day was, and I tell her about trying a few new tasks in my lessons, and she nods and smiles.

During this whole conversation, Natalie's name doesn't come up once. It's not that I want her to forget her mother, quite the opposite; should Natalie be willing, I hope she and Harper will be able to have a relationship separate from us. Only problem is, Natalie doesn't seem willing. She hasn't so much as called to see how her daughter is, and it's partly upsetting, whilst also being a relief.

Natalie is toxic. She drinks to excess, creates tension and, let's be honest, must have been having multiple affairs she probably can't even remember.

And Harper is thriving without her.

"So what do you fancy doing this evening?"

"Dunno. I've heard there's a new movie on Prime about an a capella group or something. Fancy it?"

"Sounds perfect."

We finish tea. I wash up and she dries as we listen to music, even swaying a little to the beat. Once the kitchen is sparkling again, we start the movie and settle down on the sofa.

"Oh!" I say. "I almost forgot — what about the popcorn?"

"I think we've only got microwave popcorn."

"That's fine."

I go to get up, but she puts a hand out and says, "It's all right, I'll do it."

She pushes herself up and walks to the kitchen.

I sit alone, with nothing but the distant sound of popcorn popping in the other room. A few photo frames are now displayed on the windowsill beside the television, and me and my daughter smile back at me.

I could not have imagined this life.

A month ago, the possibility of a relationship with my daughter and a home filled with happiness seemed impossible. Now we're so happy we're practically a cliché; we're the family other families envy.

And she has a friend.

And I am enjoying my job again.

And everything is just too good.

My eyes wander around the room, and I consider where we could hang some more pictures. There's a blank wall behind me, and through the open door there's blank walls throughout the hallway.

That's when I see it.

On the floor. In front of the door.

An envelope.

I look over my shoulder to see if Harper is almost finished. The popping of the popcorn is getting more frequent.

I push myself up, walk through the hallway, and I pick up the envelope.

There is no address written on the front, just my name, with the Ls curled up at the end and a heart in place of the dot above the I.

Was this hand-delivered?

I turn it over. Dig my finger beneath the flap and tear it open.

A single piece of A4 paper unfolds in my hands.

It is blank, aside from the imprint of lipstick formed by a kiss, and the words *I miss you* written below it.

I take out my phone and Google her name. Destiny Hill. The first article that comes up reads:

Teenage Girl Obsessed With Teacher Discharged From Hospital Into Police Custody

Harper returns from the kitchen with a large bowl of popcorn, and sees the look on my face. Her smile fades, and she asks me, "What's the matter?"

I go to speak, but I stutter, unable to answer.

Then I finally say, "Oh, nothing — just a bill I wasn't expecting."

"Oh. Never mind. Come watch the movie."

"I'll be one minute."

I walk into the computer room and, checking that Harper isn't watching, I place the letter and the envelope in the shredder. It gives me a sense of satisfaction to watch the paper slice into perfect strips, making the note indecipherable, and removing Destiny once again from our lives.

I resume my place on the sofa, press play on the movie, and take a handful of popcorn.

As it turns out, the movie is quite good.

And when it finishes, we say goodnight and sleep soundly in our beds, undisturbed, and for our newfound bond never to be broken again.

I have my daughter back.

And that is all that matters.

ALSO BY RICK WOOD

RICK WOOD

SHUTTER HOUSE

THIS BOOK IS FULL OF

BODIES

RICK WOOD

BLOOD SPLATTER BOOKS
18+
PSYCHO B*TCHES
Rick Wood

RICK WOOD

THE ART OF MURDER

RICK WOOD

THE SENSITIVES

www.ingramcontent.com/pod-product-compliance
Lightning Source LLC
Chambersburg PA
CBHW020919060726
47591CB00004B/1315